T0354772

Trainwreckers

David Rosten

iUniverse

TRAINWRECKERS

iUniverse books may be ordered through booksellers or by contacting:

iUniverse
1663 Liberty Drive
Bloomington, IN 47403
www.iuniverse.com
1-800-Authors (1-800-288-4677)

ISBN: 978-1-5320-0571-8 (sc)
ISBN: 978-1-5320-0570-1 (e)

Library of Congress Control Number: 2016917299

Print information available on the last page.

iUniverse rev. date: 03/15/2017

ACKNOWLEDGMENTS

My initial inspiration to do this project came while I was watching my two-year-old son play with his wooden train set. He imitated the sounds of the powerful locomotives while pushing them around the track. I later observed that same amazement over trains from my two daughters, who also delighted in toy trains.

Trainwreckers is inspired by the documented exploits of Casey Jones, Joseph S. Connolly, and William G. Crust. These turn-of-the-century characters gained fame and infamy by destroying railroad locomotives in spectacular head-on collisions, each drawing tens of thousands of frenzied, thrill-seeking spectators. The events are in the spirit of the Wild West during the late nineteenth century.

Most of the characters and incidents herein are fiction, yet they accurately reflect the bold and adventuresome spirit that once flourished in the defiant, reckless age of the steam engine.

I wish to honor my parents, Leila and Philip Rosten, and my children's great-grandmother Ione West. I dedicate this story to my children's great-great-great-grandfather Red Eagle. The story of Red Eagle was passed down from Lachlan McGillivray (1718–1799) from Inverness, Scotland. He left Scotland in search of religious freedom. He was the father of Alexander McGillivray and great-uncle to William

Weatherford (Red Eagle), who became one of the most powerful and historically important native Indian chiefs among the Creek Indians of the Southeast.

Special thanks to my children, who gave me the inspiration to complete this story.

CHAPTER 1

INDIAN TERRITORY NEAR GRAND FORKS, NORTH DAKOTA, 1953

The sun is rising, shining the early-morning light, at a funeral in progress on the prairie. It looks as if the entire Indian nation of Creeks is gathered around the simple wooden casket that rests on a wooden stand. Wood is piled high over the casket like a wooden tepee.

CH & D (Cincinnati, Hamilton and Dayton) train wreck 1896 – Photographer Wilbur Wight and Orville Wright, U.S. Library of Congress

The Creeks, dressed in tribal garb, beat their drums, and a small group of white mourners, dressed in black, look on.

A blue 1953 Pontiac Chieftain pulls up to the funeral. The car door opens, and Rachael Weatherford steps out, wearing a loose-fitting, flowing dress. She is in her late eighties, deeply lined but still completely lucid.

Her daughter, Leila Weatherford, wearing a

black dress, gets out of the car next. The men turn to gawk at this dark-haired beauty in her early thirties.

After Leila, Rachael's grandchildren, Ian and Heather, who are fraternal twins in their early teens, leap out of the backseat of the car. Ian is dressed in a button-down shirt with black pants and a small clip-on tie. Heather is wearing a black dress that matches her mother's. They are Leila's children.

The Creek chief is chanting, and suddenly he stops as if he is stepping out of a trance. He looks at the mourners and says, "We are all gathered here to honor our brother Red Eagle. Before people were on the earth, the chief of the great sky grew tired of his home in the Above World because it was always cold."

"The chief made a hole in the sky by turning a stone around and around. Through this hole, the Great Spirit of the sky gave us Red Eagle. That great sky Spirit was tired of waiting for Red Eagle to return, and now we send Red Eagle home." As he finishes his speech, he lights an oil-soaked branch and hands it to Rachael.

Rachael looks through her veil, scanning the crowd. She begins, "Friends of Red Eagle, my husband left this world a better place. I believe that he helped make this world better, not only for his family but for all Indian nations. He has helped us regain our dignity and recover our lands. He helped us by creating our tribal identity. For this we are eternally grateful."

Rachael throws the burning branch onto the pile of wood. The wood catches fire and becomes a burning inferno. Sparks and burning embers fly into the sky.

"Friends of Red Eagle, come around, all of you," she continues as she stares into the fire. "The animals and birds heard him and came. The wolf, raccoon, caribou, turtle, possum, rabbit, and squirrel." She lowers her voice. "And one day I too will come home to join you. Pass into the forever, my great warrior, lover, and friend. I will never forget you."

As the smoke rises into the sky, the chief says, "*Kwah-ee!* Put your arm around Red Eagle and make a sign. Then speak to Wind Spirit."

Just then, almost as if by magic, the winds suddenly pick up. An inferno of burning coals and embers are whipped into a funnel by the sudden winds. The winds turn into a tornado.

"*Kwah-ee*, Wind Spirit. Take Red Eagle and show him the way home."

The mourners stand there, covering their eyes against the smoke and ash, and the casket is turned into a smoldering pile of red-hot coals. The winds subside, and the smoke, coals, and embers have disappeared.

Rachael whispers to herself, "Good-bye, Red Eagle."

Heather smooths her reddish-blonde hair and says, "Come on, Grandma. It's time to go home."

Leila and the children put their arms around Rachael and walk back to their waiting car. The chief and several other Indians sit around where the burning embers were, beating their drums. They begin to magically disperse into the prairie land, the Indians and the rhythm of the drums gently fading away into nothingness.

Suddenly alone on the prairie, Leila, the children, and Rachael feel a cool wind blow. The sky is cloudy, and it is slightly windy on the plains. Winter is quickly approaching.

Ian has never asked his grandmother personal questions about her life, but now Red Eagle is gone. Ian didn't even know that his grandfather was still a member of the Indian tribe. He asks Rachael, "GG, how did you meet Red Eagle?"

Rachael is tired. It has been a long day, and she wants to curl up on her bed and bury herself in her memories. "It's a long story. Maybe another time?" says Rachael.

"Grandma, this is the time to remember Red Eagle," says Heather. "What better time is there than now? We need to hear the story before there is no one left to tell it."

Rachael looks at her grandchildren and sees genuine curiosity and interest etched on their faces. "You're right, Heather. There is no better time than the present. Come back to my house with me, and I'll tell you the story."

As they drive home, they pass an old covered wagon on the side of the road that's falling apart. On the side of the wagon are faded white letters that read "Doc Leonard and His Traveling Medicine Show."

The Pontiac Chieftain pulls into the circular driveway at Rachael's home, which is a modernized turn-of-the-century grand Victorian home in Grand Forks, North Dakota. They get out of the car and step onto the rickety wraparound porch leading to the stained glass front door.

The interior of the house is musty but has been kept tidy. An upright piano, with pictures of old Indians looking down from the top, sits quietly in the corner. The house is cluttered from the living room to the kitchen with pictures, old newspaper clippings from the turn of the century, and a heavy, bent piece of a railroad rail.

The kitchen is straight out of the 1950s, with yellow ceramic tiles, white cupboards, a green linoleum floor, and an antique Wedgewood stove and refrigerator that still work. An old, tattered Parisian hat and black-and-white photos of a beautiful woman in her twenties and a young Indian grace the mantel above the fireplace in the living room. Ian grabs a photo and asks his grandmother, "Is this you?" Rachael nods quietly without explanation as she puts away her coat.

Heather holds up a souvenir of two trains crashing into each other. She hands it to Ian. "Check this out!"

"Wow! Never seen anything like this before," he says. "Strange that GG would save this. Grandma must really be into trains."

"Grandma told me Red Eagle used to work for the railroads," says Heather. Ian puts the smashed locomotives back on the fireplace, and they head toward the door to go outside.

Rachael sits down on the sofa. "Wait a minute. Are you children ready to listen to the story of how I met your grandpa?" she asks with a mischievous look on her wrinkled face and that old twinkle in her eye. She thinks for a moment and says, "I think we should be able to put a few interesting facts together. Are you sure you have time to hear it?"

The children pause at the door, and Heather says, "Sure!"

Ian says, "Please, GG."

"As you wish. Let me get out my old diary."

Leila tells her mother that she's going home so she can work the next day. She says she's going to leave the children. Of course, Rachael says it's all right. Leila kisses Heather good night and tells her and Ian that she'll be back in a few days. And then she leaves.

Rachael struggles to get up off the couch. Heather tries to help her, but Rachael lightly slaps her hand. "I'll let you know if I need some help. Now, let's go to the kitchen."

Chuckling to herself, Heather follows GG to the kitchen and sits down with her notebook and pen. She takes out her tape recorder. "Grandma, would you mind if we tape-recorded our conversation? I'm doing a genealogy report for school. I'd like to do it on Red Eagle."

"The story isn't really that interesting," says Rachael, "but if you want to do it, it's all right."

Heather already looks a little bored, but she needs to do the report. "All right then."

Rachael makes cups of chocolate milk for them and places the cups on the breakfast table where the children are seated. She grabs her diary from the dining room and walks back to the kitchen. She blows the dust from the cover, opens the first page, and begins to read. Her hand is shaking, and her voice is barely audible.

"A horse-drawn wagon is waiting patiently at the railroad crossing."

CHAPTER 2

WESTERN TERRITORIES, 1890

A small covered wagon bears bold lettering on the side: "Doc Leonard and His Incredible Traveling Medicine Show." At the reins of this rickety sideshow on wheels are Doc Leonard and Red Eagle Weatherford.

Doc wears a tattered high hat, a tight-fitting frock coat, striped trousers, and patent leather shoes with pearl buttons. His entire wardrobe is dusty, tattered, and marked with a variety of smudges and stains.

"Step right up, ladies and gentlemen, boys and girls, in-laws, aunts and uncles, and other common household pests," Doc says in his booming voice to the crowd gathered in a small Western town. "I am here today to elucidate, educate, and enumerate a few of the priceless gems of wisdom that I have learned during my far-flung travels around the civilized world. I have here the medicines revealed by God, passed on by Indian medicine men, discovered by preachers' wives, and formulated at universities. These Indian remedies will cure the most common ailments, including baldness, asthma, and rheumatism. These remedies were passed on to me from the great Indian Red Eagle."

A townsperson from the crowd asks, "How do we know this works?"

"Have you ever seen a bald Indian?" Doc, just getting comfortable in his routine, continues. "Or an Indian with asthma or rheumatism? This medicine is guaranteed to work, or we'll send you your money back."

He looks around at the audience. "It looks like some of you don't believe me. I have here the secrets passed down by Tibetan monks. You have surely heard of the secret codes passed down by the monks during the centuries. These secrets were discovered by me. Of course, these secrets are not free."

The townspeople look skeptical.

"Have you ever seen this?" Doc takes a long metal wire, passes it through one side of his hand to the other side, and then pulls it out.

"You see? There is no blood and no pain. I received these secrets from these mystic knights."

One townsperson shouts out, "I'll take two." The rest of the

T.P & W.R.R. train wreck 1897 –
U.S. Library of Congress

townspeople gather around Doc to buy the Indian medicine.

After they have sold their Indian medicine to the last customer, Doc and Red Eagle leave the town, sitting high in the seat of the wagon and passing a bottle of "medicine" back and forth. "Red, this is the way to see the world."

They have been riding quietly for a while when Doc suddenly slumps over the reins of the wagon after drinking a little too much.

Red Eagle says, "Doc, wake up!"

The horse, black with white spots, begins to cross the train tracks without waiting for a signal from Doc. The wagon creaks over the first rail, and the horse strains in its harness to make it over the second.

Suddenly, the front wheel of the wagon shatters, and the axle crashes into the gravel between the railroad ties. Doc tumbles out of the driver's seat onto the roadbed.

"Whoa!" he says, instantly sober. "Damn!" He staggers to the wagon to retrieve his flask of medicine and puts it to his mouth for a drink but realizes the bottle is empty.

"Damn. Never seem to have the medicine when you really need it!"

He throws the empty bottle of medicine haphazardly to the ground, and it shatters. Doc looks down, sees the broken wagon wheel, and then looks at Red Eagle. "Why didn't you wake me up?"

"I did try to wake you up."

"Ah, shoot!" Doc says, disgusted.

The horse pulling the wagon looks back at Doc with an indifferent glance. "What are you looking at?" Doc says. The horse ignores him and turns around, looking away. Doc feels sorry for himself as he struggles to lift the axle and carry the wagon across the rails.

The task is hopeless. He takes his hat off, wipes sweat from his brow, and looks up at Red Eagle, who is still perched atop the wagon. "This would be a good time to help."

Red Eagle jumps off the wagon, and they attempt to move the wagon off the railroad tracks. Red Eagle is huge in stature. He wears traditional Indian clothes, and his hair is long and light reddish-brown.

"Wagon not going to move," Red Eagle says.

Doc sits down on a rail, exhausted. "Bloody hell!" He props his elbows on his knees and places his hands on his head in defeat. He shakes his head and says, "Damn. What a day."

He places his hand on the rail. "Oh no!" he cries out. Red Eagle places his ear on the rail. In disbelief, Doc says, "Just when you think it can't get worse." He jumps up and runs to his horse. "Damit!" he shouts.

"This no good, Doc."

Doc pulls Damit by the reins, trying to pull the cart over the tracks. "Damit! Come on. Oh, damnation!" He looks up and sees smoke from the stacks of the oncoming freight train. "Uh-oh." He rushes back to the wagon and tries to lift the axle again. The wagon doesn't budge.

Meanwhile, inside the cab of the racing freight train, the engineer sees the horse and wagon on the train tracks. He yells to the fireman, "Look at this up ahead."

The fireman looks ahead and sees the wagon stuck on the tracks. "Let's get it!" he says. He begins shoveling more coal into the steam boilers, and the train begins to pick up more speed. The fireman is covered with black soot from the burning coals. His blue eyes stand out on his soot-covered face. There is no hint of alarm in his eyes, only amusement.

"You think he'll get it unhitched in time?" the fireman asks, watching the wagon only several hundred yards ahead.

The engineer laughs. "Not if I can help it." He opens up the throttle, and the train picks up even more speed.

Doc frantically races back to unharness his horse. "They're not even slowing down!" He looks over his shoulder and sees that the train is actually speeding up. "Red, this is it!"

Red mumbles to himself.

"Damn. Damn them. What's the matter with people these days?" asks Doc.

"I always said that when white man was shooting at me and my family," replies Red.

"Damit. Come on, Damit. We gotta get you outta here," Doc says to his horse.

The train runners pound like thunder on the tracks. The smokestack belches a plume of sparks as long as a comet's tail.

The engineer smiles and says, "Five dollars says he don't make it!"

The fireman laughs. "You're on!"

They both let out a shout. "Yahoo!"

The fireman frantically stokes the fires as the train whistle roars.

At the last instant before the locomotive smashes into his wagon, Doc unhitches his horse. "Scat, Damit!" He swats Damit on his hind end. "Go on now, shoo, Damit!"

The horse barely makes it across the tracks, inches away from the speeding locomotive. The locomotive plows into the covered wagon and shatters it into kindling wood. To avoid the exploding debris from the wagon, Doc and Red Eagle leap headfirst into a nearby trench. The train roars past with pieces of the wagon's canvas streaming from the side of the train engine.

Doc and Red Eagle look up from the trench and see both the fireman and the engineer looking back. The fireman waves to them and laughs.

Doc yells, "Just who do you think you are, running over decent common folk?" Doc wheels about and spots his Winchester rifle lying between the rails. He runs to the gun and picks it up. He tells Red Eagle, "Maybe I'll get a lucky shot!" He works the bolt action and fires wildly at the retreating caboose.

Inside the steam locomotive, the engineer and fireman are hysterical with laughter. The fireman tells the engineer, "You should have seen their faces!"

Their fun is short-lived. One of Doc's shots shatters the window, knocking over the kerosene lantern in the caboose. The fireman asks the engineer, "You hear something?"

"What's going on back there?" the engineer says. They look back at the caboose in astonishment.

The fireman shouts, "The caboose is on fire! We have to stop the train before the gorge."

The engineer pulls back on the brake. "Hang on!" The train comes to a screeching halt in the center of the trestle over a deep gorge.

"The whole damn thing is burning. I'm gonna let the steam outta the engine," the fireman says.

The two railroaders race to the rear of the train. The caboose is now engulfed in flames.

"Help me uncouple the caboose!" the fireman calls.

The engineer grabs a wrench. By this time, the flames are shooting out the sides of the caboose.

The railroad men struggle to uncouple the caboose from the train. The flames are too intense, and the fire is spreading to the next car.

The fireman is frantic. He says, "We can't get close enough. We gotta unhook this car!" They race to the back of the next car to free the coupling pin.

Doc and Red Eagle are running along the tracks. Doc has his Winchester in his hand and catches up with the train. He runs onto the trestle and glances down at the swiftly moving river below. He watches the fireman and engineer struggling with the pin.

"Y'all need some help?" Doc says with a look of satisfaction sweeping over his face.

They look up at Doc but carry on with their business.

Doc says, "I've got some kindling wood back down the road. We could make a fire for a barbeque." He sits on the rails and laughs as he watches the fire begin to consume another car.

The trainmen ignore Doc and tend to the task at hand.

The engineer says, "Hurry! Get me some steam."

"There's none left! We ain't gonna make it," the fireman tells him.

On the burning train, the engineer says, "We don't have enough time. We'd better uncouple some of the other cars." The railroad men uncouple three cars ahead and allow the others to burn.

The men look up and see a passenger train bearing down on the burning freight train. The passenger train's wheels lock and reverse, sending a shower of sparks off the rails and raining down into the rapids of the river below.

Red Eagle runs down the track and shouts for Doc. The smile vanishes from Doc's face as the 505 local train roars around the bend onto the trestle from behind him.

The trainmen panic as they see the train coming down the tracks, and they race back to the locomotive cab to try to get the locomotive rolling.

Doc screams, "Sweet Jesus, Mary, and Joseph! What's going on around here?" He runs toward Red Eagle. "Jump, Red. Jump, you fool!"

The train is right on Red Eagle's heels. At the last second he jumps, and the train continues down the track.

Doc knows that the passenger train is going to rear-end the burning freight train. He looks down at the river below and makes a spectacular leap from the trestle into the raging river below.

He surfaces just in time to see the freight locomotive and its cars smashed from behind by the passenger train.

The burning freight cars jackknife off the tracks and fall, end over end, into the gorge, taking half the trestle timbers with it.

The passenger train comes to a complete stop on the trestle.

Doc is swept downstream by the current. He grabs onto a rock near the side of the river, desperately trying to keep his head above water. He looks back, sees a boxcar bearing down on him in the churning rapids, and swims to safety behind some boulders.

The boxcar is diverted, barely missing Doc as it crashes into the boulders and breaks apart. The floating debris and timbers float innocently downstream.

CHAPTER 3

At a gypsy camp beside the river, a group of gypsies sits around a fire in their multicolored outfits, playing songs about the old country they came from. They look up from their singing and see Doc jump from the trestle. Several of them gasp as the trains explode in front of their eyes, and a few scream. They stop singing, and someone points up at the trestle, claiming he saw someone jump, wondering if anyone else saw it.

Doc struggles to pull himself onto the riverbank, bruised and battered from his fall into the river. When he is finally on land, he stops moving. He doesn't appear to be breathing, and his eyes are closed.

Rachael, the gypsy king's daughter, a redhead in her early twenties, tentatively approaches Doc, while others grab the booty from the train washing up on the shore and carry it away.

"Papa, hurry! There's a dead man here!" she calls.

Luther rushes to her and checks Doc's wrist for a pulse. "I don't think he's dead," he says and pushes down on Doc's stomach.

Gypsy woman – National Photo Company Collection

He rolls Doc over to his side, and Doc coughs up water. Then he opens his eyes and sits up.

"Where in God's name?" he says. Doc looks around, sees the flickering lights from lanterns, and catches the somber faces of the gypsies and their families.

Luther looks at him with pity and says, "Here, son, let me help you."

Doc quickly sees that these people are gypsies. They are all dressed in tattered clothes. The women wear long dresses, and the men all sport mustaches.

"The Lord has helped me enough for one day, I think," Doc says, laughing.

Luther puts his arm around Doc's waist and helps him up the side of the riverbank. He tells the gypsies, "This man is our guest. It is our duty to take care of him until he can recover from his wounds."

Luther helps Doc sit down by the fire. All eyes are on Rachael. She says, "Let me get you some dry clothes."

When she returns, Rachael offers Doc a cup of coffee. "I'm all right," he says, and he looks around for Red Eagle but doesn't see him. "Did anyone see if anyone else survived the crash?"

Luther says to Doc, "We saw him jump with you, but we haven't seen anyone else that survived the fall."

Everyone turns as they hear someone running from the woods, screaming. A young gypsy girl yells, "Help, there's an Indian after me." Red Eagle breaks through the bushes after her with blood streaming down the side of his forehead. He makes a formidable sight.

"Don't panic! That's my friend," Doc says, beginning to figure out what this group is all about.

Doc begins to speak in an authoritarian, oratorical manner that shows he knows how to handle a crowd of gawking people, but he can't get his words out. "Uh … yes, well … uh, ahem." He clears his throat. "It does indeed seem that on this day God decided to save me and this savage Indian as one of his flock of beloved children. The Lord saved us from the clutches of death and the fiery pits that might have awaited us in hell. Perhaps He sent an angel down to rescue us from an eternal life of damnation. But when it comes right down to it, there is no other possible explanation for our being saved other than it being a miracle from the Lord!"

The gypsy crowd is hushed with excitement as Doc speaks. It is obvious that Doc knows how to work a crowd with his charisma and keep them captivated.

Luther looks at a couple of faces that are absorbed in Doc's speech. He is intrigued. "Tell us more."

Doc is totally worked up and talking rapidly. He's on a roll. "There I was, stuck to the train tracks after the axle on my wagon broke, carrying supplies to the local orphanage, when suddenly I heard a train. I bent my ear down close to the shiny steel rail and heard a most frightening sound. I could see its billowing stacks of smoke steaming from the top! I had nowhere to turn except to the Lord! And then, from the same direction, another train was quickly approaching!

"The train was rapidly speeding toward me. They were about to collide with each other, with me in the middle! They were fast as a bullet, and I thought I was a goner—when I saw the light. A most divine light! It shone down on me, a heavenly stream of sunlight filled with the music of angels playing trumpets. Then a voice said unto me, 'Doc Leonard, it's time to jump!'

"Well, now, if a heavenly voice is speaking to you, whether it's convenient for you or not, you listen! And the voice came at such an opportune moment that I listened. But first, I had to warn this noble savage to jump too. He too is one of God's creatures. And then, jump we did. We leaped from the bridge and were flying through the air! And just as we were about to be speared upon the jagged rocks below the surface of the water, the Lord's hand caught us and gently placed us in the river. And there I knew, even as I fought the rushing rapids and struggled to breathe with water all around me, that the Lord had saved me for some special purpose."

The crowd is completely silent. Everyone is staring at Doc in total awe of his close encounter with death and his personal contact with the Lord.

Luther breaks the silence. His eyes are lit up like little torches. "Well, go on then, brother, what purpose have you come to fulfill in God's name?"

Doc has a dramatic finish. "The good Lord wanted me, a lowly commoner, a humble and honest man, to spread His word throughout this great land of ours!"

Some of the gypsies begin cheering and clapping, and most are talking among themselves. This is the most exciting story that some of the gypsies have ever heard. They can't believe that anyone could have survived that train collision, but a person has been saved—and he has spoken to God while doing it.

Luther tells the crowd, "Everyone, what say you to inviting this brave soldier and the Indian savage on our march to save others from a lifetime of evil vices and an eternity in purgatory?"

The gypsies nod their heads in agreement. Luther nods and tells Doc, "We'd like you to accompany us, brother, as we travel across these territories."

"I've got to leave," Doc says. "I'm going to California to start a new life. The Lord has assisted me already and has saved me. I know that the work of the Lord is never finished."

Luther is slightly startled, caught off guard by the answer. "But your story is one that needs to be heard! I mean, you just escaped death and were saved by the everlasting grace of God!"

Doc, feeling that he may not be able to leave, looks uncomfortable. "Your, uh, gracious offer to stay is compelling. How long would you, uh, propose that you would require our services?"

Doc whispers to Red Eagle, "We've got to get out of here. These people are nuts."

"You're welcome to leave at any time. But surely you would want to fulfill the promise you made to God as he spared your life!"

"Well, uh, of course. I just, uh, thought I'd venture out into the territories with Red Eagle is all—to spread the word. I mean, the Lord didn't say anything about joining a group or nothin'. I must leave you and retrieve my faithful horse." Doc starts to back away slowly from the group.

"So be it, then," says Luther, looking suspicious. "We'll send a few escorts with you to retrieve your horse."

"Come on, Red Eagle, we're leaving now," Doc says.

"I am tired. No travel tonight."

"I'll see you in a few, Injun." Doc prepares to leave the camp with several gypsies and search along the riverbank to find his horse.

Rachael follows. She has seen this before with her father. She tells Doc, "I think my father plans to keep you for a while."

"I will always be grateful to him for saving my life," Doc says.

Rachael bows her head and goes back to the fire circle.

After Doc finds Damit, he is escorted back to the gypsy camp, where the group is playing music once again. He is led into the tent where Rachael is tending to Red Eagle's head wounds. Doc asks him, "How are you feeling?"

"Head hurt."

"Well, it appears that we are going to be staying here for a while."

Red Eagle winks and inclines his head toward Rachael, whose voluptuous features are almost falling out of her low-cut top. "This isn't so bad. Red Eagle stay here."

Just then, Luther enters the tent. He asks Doc, "Have you decided if you will travel with us?"

"Your offer to stay is compelling," Doc says noncommittally, having a sinking feeling that he will not be able to leave by his own free will.

"Again, you're welcome to leave at any time, brother. Of course, if you stay, you will be paid a modest sum for each of your appearances. And we have to save the soul of that Indian savage too."

"Of course we will accept your generous offer, brother," Doc says. "This will be a labor of love, and you don't have to pay me to do the Lord's work."

"I'm certain that your account of the train collision will become more convincing each time it's heard. A terrifying way to come to work for the Lord, but I must say, I would have paid five dollars to hear what happened with those two trains and how you were saved."

Doc is filled with inspiration as the gypsy music continues playing outside the tent.

CHAPTER 4

Later that night, Doc enters Red Eagle's tent. Red Eagle is sleeping, with bandages on his head. Doc shakes him. "Wake up. We're going to get out of here."

Red Eagle wakes up and says, "What are you doing? These are nice people, Doc."

"Are you crazy, Red Eagle? We've gotta get outta here."

"I stay here."

"Your head injury has really affected you, Red. If you haven't guessed, if we don't make a break now, these people won't let us go."

Red Eagle at the White House (far right)
1923 – U.S. Library of Congress

"I stay, Doc. You leave."

Doc gives in. Red Eagle is more stubborn than he is. "Okay, Red Eagle, I'll stay for a little while. Then I'm out of here."

In the morning, the gypsies leave the place where they have been staying and travel down the dusty road in their wagons. Doc and Red Eagle sit in the back of a wagon, and Damit is tied up next to the wagon.

"I've got to leave soon, Red," Doc says. "My parents were traveling circus performers. They never amounted to anything. My father was a drunk, and one day my mother just got up and left us. Never saw her again. Afterward, I told my father I'd make it to California someday. My father was a real warm guy. All he said was good-bye. And that was it. Never saw my father again either."

Red Eagle says, "You lucky, Doc. At least you didn't see your parents shot in front of you. I never saw my parents again. I never said good-bye. I just ran, and I'm still running."

Doc hangs his head. "Looks like our new road show has begun," he says as the gypsy troupe pulls into the next town.

CHAPTER 5

Several days later, Doc is doing his first testimonial speech up on a stage. Red Eagle is sitting next to him, his head still bandaged. Doc, finishing his speech, says to the onlookers, "And that is the way that the Lord spoke to me. He said, 'Save the soul of this Injun.' Give us your generous contributions so that he may be saved and we can speak directly to the Lord for you. Give generously from your heart. Thank you, my brothers."

Luther gets up on the stage and talks to his followers. "Please give generously so we can continue the Lord's work. Let the Lord into your heart!"

The townspeople sing gospel music while the hat is being passed around.

Doc's eyes are trained on the hat, which is overflowing with money, and he whispers to Red Eagle, "I'm leaving town tonight for California. You're welcome to come with me."

"I'm staying, Doc. I don't understand it myself, but this is where I belong."

"So be it, Red. Look me up if you're heading out west."

"You've been good to me, Doc. We'll see each other again."

CHAPTER 6

In the middle of the night, Doc Leonard, newly initiated servant of the Lord, sneaks into Luther's tent where the money is kept. A few minutes later he exits the tent.

He gently stuffs his saddlebags with handfuls of money. As Doc mounts his horse, a voice calls out from the brush.

Rachael and Luther step out. Several other gypsies come out behind them.

Luther says, "And what have you in those saddlebags, Doc?"

Doc looks at the group. One of them is holding the bridle of his horse. They have him red-handed. He tries to act cool but is scared to death.

Rachael whispers to Luther, "I don't want him to go, Dad."

Doc clears his throat. "It is time for me to leave. I cannot express in words the depth of my gratitude nor thank you enough for your compassionate nature, but …" He tries to think of some explanation quickly. "I'm thinking of starting my own ministry. And so I must go. G'night!"

U.S. Library of Congress

21

Luther doesn't understand the urgency. He says, "Surely you don't have enough food or provisions for a very long journey. And a long journey it must be, my friend. Rachael, get a few things for our friend's journey." He motions to Rachael, and Doc is stunned but manages to keep his cool. "While we are most sad to see your departure, you must go on a long journey so that your work will not interfere with ours."

Rachael returns and gives Doc some provisions. "We have packed food and clothing—and twenty dollars, to boot—for your journey."

Doc starts to feel a little guilty. "I want to thank you all for your generous offer to stay, but I cannot accept this. It is too kind."

Luther smiles warmly. "Then you must go. Have a safe journey."

Doc waves back to Luther and Rachael. Once clear of their encampment, Doc breaks into a full gallop. He still feels a twinge of guilt, but not enough to keep him from riding to the nearest junction and out to California.

CHAPTER 7

OMAHA, NEBRASKA

A short time later, Doc has made it to an old train depot. At the ticket counter, Doc says, "I'd like to purchase a ticket for me and my horse on the next train to San Francisco."

"That'll be twenty dollars," the ticket clerk tells him. "The train will be leaving in three hours from platform two." Doc hands him the money, and the clerk gives Doc the ticket in return.

"Have a good trip. Take your horse to the boxcar."

Doc gathers his saddlebags, throws them over his shoulder, and makes his way down the depot platform—and stops.

A young lady in the crowd grabs Doc's attention, and he realizes it's Rachael. Red Eagle is following close behind with his head still bandaged.

Doc tries to hide behind the ticket counter. As he continues to watch Rachael, he realizes how beautiful she is. She is stunning with her shining red hair. Rachael gives Doc a single glance and suddenly realizes it's him.

Doc attempts to back up to avoid being seen, but it's too late. He takes off, running down the platform. Rachael shouts, "Stop him! Stop that man. He's stolen our money!"

People turn around as Doc runs by them. The conductor hears the commotion and steps off the train. As Doc is running by, the conductor puts his leg out and trips him. Doc goes flying down the platform. Onlookers grab Doc and hold him down. Red Eagle and Rachael make their way through the crowd to Doc.

New Haven wrecked train 1913 – Bain Collection - U.S. Library of Congress

Doc looks up at them with a smile and says, "Fancy running into you both."

Rachael says, "You stole our money, Doc, and we want it back."

The constable comes rushing out of the station and heads over to the scene. He nods toward Doc, who is struggling, and tells the conductor, "Good job, sir."

"All in a day's work," the conductor says, touching the tip of his hat.

The constable asks, "What are the charges against this man?"

"This man stole our money, and we're going to get it back," Rachael tells him.

Doc pleads with the constable, "I didn't steal any money."

"Why don't we let the judge decide? I'm taking you to jail," the constable says as he pulls Doc up roughly by his arm.

"Jail? What are the charges?"

As the constable drags him off in handcuffs, Doc tells Red Eagle, "Red, get Damit. He's still on the train. And take care of my bags."

"Don't worry, Doc. I get your things."

CHAPTER 8

Later that day, Red Eagle tells Rachael, "I think we should go see him," Red Eagle tells her.

"Why would I want to see him? I'll see him in court."

Red Eagle, who knows Doc pretty well, says, "What good is it to see him in court? You'll never see your money."

Rachael thinks about it for a moment. "Did you look in his bags?"

"Why would I do that?"

"Because he has our money," she tells him.

"Then I would be like Doc. Untrustworthy."

"Then I'll check the bag myself."

"You have the whole world to see. Doc only has his little bag."

Rachael huffs and sticks out her hand. "Give me Doc's bag."

Red Eagle refuses to turn over the bag. "I gave Doc my promise. I take care of Doc's bag."

Rachael sees that she won't get anywhere with Red Eagle. "Then let's go see Doc."

CHAPTER 9

The Omaha City Jail is a little, one-room, wooden jailhouse in the middle of a bustling cow town. Doc is sitting in a small cell just behind the front desk.

Rachael tells the jailer, "I'd like to see the prisoner."

He looks around and replies, "We have so many prisoners. Which one do you want to see?"

Rachael glares at him. "You know which one."

The jailer smirks. "Whom may I say is calling, miss?"

"Stop it with the funny business. I want to see the prisoner in private. He has his rights, and if you don't comply immediately, I'm going to see the judge."

"A little on edge, are we? Well, don't worry yourself, miss. You can speak with the prisoner alone. I'll step outside. No funny business."

After the jailer steps outside, Doc asks, "Why are you here?"

"I thought you'd be happy to see us," she says curtly.

"Look at the mess you've gotten me into."

"I didn't put you in this mess."

"I just borrowed the money. I was planning to pay it back."

Rachael shakes her head. "You were planning on disappearing with it."

Doc turns to Red Eagle and asks, "Did you get my horse and bag?"

"Of course we got the horse for you," Rachael answers. To test him, she says, "I'm keeping the bag, since the contents belong to me!"

Doc relents. "Then why are you here? Are you planning on getting me out?"

"I'm going to let the judge decide," she says and crosses her arms across her chest.

"You can have what's in the bag."

"Nice of you to offer, since it already *belongs to us*. We have your bag. Your number is up."

Doc levels with her. "I don't really care about the money. What I really need is a partner."

"Who would want to be a partner with the likes of you?" she says.

"I have this great plan, and it will make the money I borrowed from you look like it's nothing."

"I have the money. What do you have to offer?" she says, uncrossing her arms and leaning closer. She looks at Red Eagle, and he shrugs.

Doc tells her, "The chance to make yourself famous."

"No, thank you, Doc. I'm out of here. Thanks for the money back." She turns to leave.

U.S. Library of Congress

"Okay, you win. I'm sorry."

"That's better. What's your idea?" She says it with a smile as she turns to face him again.

"We're going to wreck trains."

"You're crazy, Doc. See ya later."

"Don't leave me here. Just give me one chance to prove myself. Then I'm off to California."

"You have your train wreck," Rachael says. "You're partners with both Red Eagle and me."

"With Red Eagle? He's an Indian."

"I wouldn't be here except for Red Eagle. He's watching out for me, and that's what my papa told him to do."

"Then partners it is. How about the money?"

"I don't know about the money, Doc. We never looked in your bag."

"Why didn't you look in my bag and take the money?"

"'Cause then I'd be like you, and I never want to be like you."

"I swear it, Rachael, you made a good decision."

"I hope so. My papa wants that money back."

"Well, get me out of here, and I'll pay your papa back with interest."

"I'll get the jailer," she says.

"What are you doing?"

"I'm getting you out of here."

Rachael walks through the jailhouse door. "I want this man released," she says to the jailer.

The jailer walks back into the jailhouse and says, "I can't release this prisoner."

"This man is falsely imprisoned," Rachael says. "I'm the only witness. If I don't show up in court, there is no evidence, and then we'll look to receive money from you and your city for false imprisonment. Say good-bye to your job too."

"Let me look at this file," he says as he sits behind his desk and opens up the file. "Looks like you're right. I need you to sign here that we're releasing this prisoner to you."

Rachael signs the paper, and the jailer tells her, "You sure are smart, lady. You sure you're not a lawyer or something?"

"Been in a few courthouses."

The jailer unlocks the cell door. "Take it easy."

"Yeah, see ya around." Doc walks out of the jailhouse with Rachael and Red Eagle. He tells her, "You're going to be a good partner."

Later in the day, they get Damit and make their way to a locomotive foundry.

CHAPTER 10

FOUNDRY, OMAHA, NEBRASKA, 1891

Doc walks across the train yard tracks to the locomotive foundry. He begins to shop for locomotives with Rachael and Red Eagle.

The foundry shop is a great, wide shack with the sun pouring in through the open door and windows all around. Clouds of dust and red-hot metal filings dance in the light. The place is full of the sound of hammering and the grunts and shouts of men wrestling with heavy locomotive parts. The floor is cluttered with headlights, brass trimmings of engines, flat wheels, and dismembered boilers.

Doc is arrogant, walking among these giant hulks, knowing that he is capable of buying a locomotive with such power.

Wrecking Man, owner of the foundry, addresses Doc in a high-pitched voice that doesn't exactly match his huge body and bald head. "What can I do for you?"

Doc says, "I'm looking for a good locomotive."

Wrecking Man says, "Look around, partner, and tell me when you find one that looks interesting."

Doc tells him thanks, and he continues to walk around the foundry. Looking at a dilapidated locomotive, he says, "How much is this one?"

"You have a good eye for locomotives. Five hundred dollars."

Doc nods. "I'm going to look around some more."

"Look around some more, but you won't find a better one for this price."

Doc thinks to himself and then says, "Mm-hmm, I reckon I'd better look around a bit."

He continues to walk around and inspect the locomotives. He gets up on one to inspect the interior of a furnace. He peers inside and then turns to see Red Eagle with a frown on his face.

"What are you looking at?"

Red Eagle is covered with soot and grease on his unshaven face. He's wearing an old, greasy pair of denim overalls. "Not this one."

"Why?"

Red Eagle points to the furnace. "Because the furnace has at least a dozen holes in it." He glances inside the furnace briefly, and then gives Doc an impatient look. "Those are heat flues. With those holes, you can't heat the boiler."

Doc gives Red Eagle a sheepish look. He tries to figure out what he is talking about. "What's the difference? We plan to smash it up."

"With what? This locomotive won't even move."

"How do you know so much about trains?"

Red Eagle is bewildered. "I learned about the white man's horse long ago. This iron horse destroyed my people. It was the railroads that stole our Indian lands. The railroads have made my life miserable ever since. The railroads killed my parents and have my people living on reservations. The reservation is like prison to us."

"Do you know how to run a locomotive?"

"Listen, Doc. Do I know how to run the white man's iron horse? The white man has taken my land for their railroads and all the land for ten miles on both sides of the rail. The white man took our buffalo and shot them for fun. My Indian brothers had nothing to eat. We starved on our own land."

He stares at Doc who is listening sympathetically. Calmly and with conviction, he continues, "I'll wear your war paint. I'll drive your train and crash it. I will make my family proud!"

Doc laughs. "Okay, partner, but remember, this is show business, and we get paid for it. Now, help me find a good engine to smash."

"Who would want to pay to see a thing like that besides me?" Red Eagle asks.

"Lots of people, I hope. Remember: give the audience what it wants. Deep down within the soul of every decent person is the uncontrollable desire to see things smashed up."

"Doc, we'd better not stay around here too long. People will think we're all a little touched in the head." The duo continues to walk through the train yard, shopping for an old locomotive.

Red Eagle comes to a train and stops. "This is the one to buy. All the rest are junk. We can pick up another locomotive at the works in Lincoln."

Doc walks up to Wrecking Man. "That is the locomotive we want. We also need the coal car and caboose."

Wrecking Man says, "That'll be seven hundred and fifty dollars."

Doc peels the money from a wad of bills. "Here's the five hundred dollars."

Wrecking Man counts the money. "You're a tough negotiator. Deal. Now you can take the locomotive and leave."

Doc tells Red Eagle and Rachael, "You two, get in."

Red Eagle looks at Doc and hesitates before boarding. "Doc, I must warn you about this show of yours. The railroads will not like it. Show or no show, smashing trains will make them look bad."

"Don't worry, Injun. I can handle it. Now get in."

Red Eagle looks up the steps of the locomotive cab like it is a holy monument. The train consists of an aging Baldwin 4-4-0 locomotive, coal tender, and a battered caboose, all built in the 1870s. He slowly climbs the steps and brings his giant frame under the roof and into the cab. He reaches out to touch the rusty throttle lever and gazes at the pressure gauges covered with cobwebs. His gaze meets Doc's smiling eyes.

"Congratulations, Injun," Doc says. "You are now chief engineer."

Red Eagle becomes teary-eyed. He stays silent, unable to find words to suit the moment.

"Are you sure you know how to operate the locomotive?"

"Sure," Red Eagle answers with a wide grin.

Red Eagle handles the locomotive like an expert engineer. However, he has difficulty with yard procedures. Switching and right-of-way maneuvering are all new to him. The train engine goes through a blinking red light in his attempt to get out of the train yard.

Doc says, "Hey, what are you doing?"

The train backs into a coal car on the tracks. A large cloud of black coal dust appears.

Doc and Red Eagle are covered with soot, and Rachael, looking on, laughs.

"Sorry, boss. You okay?" Red Eagle says.

Doc nods. "I'm fine. I just hope you didn't do too much damage."

Red Eagle is amused. As he jumps out of the cab to inspect the damage, he says, "Don't worry, boss. If engine was damaged, we'd know. The boilers would have exploded!"

"Well, *that's* comforting."

Red Eagle moves the train forward and leaves the foundry area. As they are moving along on the straight tracks, Red Eagle motions with his hands to Doc. "Doc, I think I've got the hang of this."

"I don't like the way you say *hang*."

Just at that moment, the train derails, and two dozen cursing yardmen come running toward them. They are all covered with grease. A yardman shouts, "What in God's name are you doing? You almost killed us!"

"We're trying to wreck the train, of course," Doc says.

The yardman glares at Doc. "Very funny, mister. We gotta get your locomotive back on the rails and get ya outta here."

The yardmen attempt to get the train back on the rails, and one of them jumps into the cab and moves the train forward so the front wheels rise on a dolly. He slaps his hands together. "That's it. Good luck!" Under his breath he mumbles, "You'll need it," as he jumps off the train.

Doc, Red Eagle, and Rachael look out the window and wave good-bye.

CHAPTER 11

Train cab, Omaha, Nebraska

R ed Eagle is back in the cab and going along the straightaway in their aging Baldwin 4-4-0 locomotive. He doesn't say a word. He is afraid to look in Doc's direction since the derailment.

Doc finally breaks the silence. "Do you read?"

"Sorry, no," Red Eagle says, shaking his head.

"That was close, Injun. One more mess-up like that and you're through."

"*You're* through, Doc, if you threaten him again," Rachael says. "He's your partner, and you will treat him like a partner."

"You're right. I'm just not used to having an Indian as my partner."

They leave the Omaha city limits. Doc is sitting in the cab, studying the timetables provided to them, acting as a navigator since Red Eagle doesn't know how to read.

"Why didn't you tell me you didn't know how to read, Injun?" Doc asks.

"You never asked."

"I'm going to teach him to read," Rachael says, smiling at Red Eagle.

Red Eagle shrugs his shoulders, seemingly a little embarrassed. "Fine."

"You don't say much, do you?" Doc asks with annoyance in his voice.

"I have learned to keep quiet. When I speak, I am not always heard."

"How'd you learn to operate a train if you don't know how to read?" Doc asks him.

"I have been dealing with railroads for a very long time."

"You're not answerin' my question."

"My father was a white man."

"What!" Doc says, his eyes wide and mouth gaping.

Red Eagle matter-of-factly replies, "My father was Scottish. He owned a supply store. Then he married my mother, a Creek Indian princess squaw. He tried to help fight the white men.

"He believed that the white men were wrong in what they were doing, that they had lost their souls long ago. He was a good man for what he did."

"So, I daresay you have a family tradition of this sort of thing?" Doc asks.

Red Eagle sighs heavily. "When the railroads came to my land, it hurt us very much. They did not ask to build on our land. They did not respect the land. They drove spikes deep into the ground where generations were buried, where we had homes and held sacred rituals. They put their iron horses on these rails. Black smoke rose from them for miles around. It was the railroads that stole these lands from my tribe."

"This doesn't have anything to do with our work," Doc says quietly.

"The white man took my land for their railroads. Then he could not stop. He took our buffalo and shot them for fun. We were starving on our own land. They took away our pride, our honor. They left us with nothing. They found they did not need us, so they began shooting us for fun, like the buffalo."

Doc has gone quiet, a concerned and sympathetic expression on his face.

"I warn you, boss, they are not going to like you crashing their trains."

"Don't worry. We'll be fine."

They approach a steep downgrade. Red Eagle stands up, noticing something about the train. He knows the train is gaining too much speed. He yells to Doc, "The wheel brake on the caboose, Doc—turn it to slow down the train before we hit the curve."

Doc turns and sees the approaching curve. He makes his way to the rear and cranks the rusty wheel until it will turn no farther. Doc makes his way back to the front of the train and into the cab. "I tightened the brakes all the way down," he yells over the noise of the engine.

Red Eagle nods his head and says, "Good!"

They round the curve and set off on a level straightaway, all breathing a sigh of relief that a disaster has been averted.

"Something is wrong," Red Eagle says a few moments later. "The engine seems sluggish. We are barely making twenty miles an hour."

He gives it more throttle, but little speed, if any, is gained. "I'm going to stop the train and look for the problem. Train not running right."

After Red Eagle stops the train, the three of them jump down from the locomotive and walk back to look at the wheels of the caboose, looking for the problem. Smoke is coming off the wheels. There is a metallic smell in the air. Red Eagle stops at the caboose and stares at the rear wheels.

"There's our problem, Doc," he says, gesturing with his head toward the wheels. "You turned the wheel brake so tightly that all four wheels locked and skidded for five miles along the rails. The wheels are worn down halfway to their axles and now resemble four flat tires." Red Eagle looks at him. "I thought you knew what you were doing."

Rachael looks at the wheels of the train. "You guys are a sad group. Our business is going to be bankrupt before we begin."

"Do not worry. This train is going to be just fine," Doc says.

"Doc, you turned the wheel brake so tight that the wheels couldn't turn at all. These wheels are worn down to their axles," Rachael says, nearly in a panic. Her accusatory glare goes unnoticed by Doc.

"At least we're ten miles closer to our destination," Red Eagle says. Then he turns and gets back to the cab.

Doc doubles over with laughter. "Now what do we do, Injun?"

"We unlock the brakes and you ride in the caboose the rest of the way to Lincoln. Then we get the wheels repaired. I drive the train."

"Sounds good, partner. Then we're heading west, out to Denver."

Red Eagle gets the train moving again, and Doc's caboose bumps and jolts along the rails.

From his cab, Red Eagle stares up at the sky. "Spirit of the sky, white man pays me for wrecking the white man's iron horse? I know that you have a bigger purpose for me. I just don't see it yet."

CHAPTER 12

Lincoln, Nebraska

The locomotive pulls into the train works. The yardmen laugh when they see the caboose. As Doc steps down from the caboose, a yardman asks him, "What can I do for you?"

"I need some used steel wheels for the caboose."

The man smiles at him. "I couldn't see that. We've got some extra wheels. We can get you fixed up pretty quick, but it's going to cost you."

"Thanks."

*Fort Worth & Denver railway
1918 – U.S. Library of Congress*

"You guys take a walk around Lincoln. I think you'll enjoy our capital of Nebraska."

"Much obliged," Doc says, tipping his hat.

Doc turns to Rachael and Red Eagle. In a hushed voice, he asks, "Red Eagle, would you stay and keep an eye on things? Rachael, why don't you and I walk around Lincoln?"

"Sounds like a good idea," Red Eagle says. Rachael nods and follows Doc out of the foundry.

Several minutes later, the yardmen begin working on the caboose. Two yardmen, Hank and Gus, walk to the back of the caboose and open the back door.

"Let's check out what they have in here," Hank says as they enter the caboose.

Gus looks around outside before closing the door behind him. "Yeah, but make it quick."

"Coast is clear. It's a little dark in here," says Hank.

Out of the shadows, Red Eagle rises up, towering over the yardmen. "Lost?"

The yardmen fall backward onto the floor of the caboose, scared out of their wits. "Aaaaah!" Hank yells.

"Don't hurt us, Injun," Gus says. "We didn't do nothin'. Good time to fix the wheels."

"Yeah," Hank says as he gets to his feet, backing away from Red Eagle with his hands raised slightly. Red Eagle remains silent, glaring at them. Hank and Gus turn and run out of the caboose.

Doc and Rachael walk along the streets of Lincoln where law and order thrive. Well-dressed people with their children pass by them with looks of disgust on their faces. Doc looks at his reflection in a shop's window. "Guess I look pretty shabby," he says, laughing.

Rachael laughs with him and says, "This is a beautiful town. One day I'd like to settle down in a town like this."

"Looks nice, but not for me. I'm heading out to California. That is the land of opportunity."

"Don't you ever think of settling down someday?"

"Never thought that far ahead. Until I'm in California, I'm just rolling from one town to the next."

"I'll look you up someday when I'm out there," says Rachael. "Maybe you can show me around."

"Sure."

"You're a hard guy to get to know," she says and stops walking.

Doc stops beside her. "What's there to know? You want small talk?"

Rachael doesn't say a word.

Doc tells her, "I grew up in the circus. My pa trained the lions. My ma flew on the trapeze, until one day she flew the coop! I'd seen everything by the time I was ten. When I was fifteen, I told my pa good-bye. He said bye. I took Damit, and that's the end of the story."

"You didn't have any love in your life."

"And I still don't know what love is." He looks down and shuffles a foot on the dusty road. "We'd better be getting back."

"Yeah," she says with a tentative smile.

When they reach the train, everything is repaired and ready to go.

Doc shakes the yardman's hand and says, "Looks good. We're heading to Denver."

They climb aboard, and the train begins to move out of the foundry.

CHAPTER 13

Denver, 1891

Doc, Red Eagle, and Rachael arrive in Denver, which is one of the many overnight boomtowns to spring up at Union Pacific Railroad stops. They have decided that they needed to stage their first train wreck in Denver. Denver has lots of gold, and occasionally vigilantes take over. Murder is commonplace. Keno and Monte players operate their games in dimly lit tents. Razorback hogs and scrawny cattle wallow in mudholes on the main street. There are almost as many people in the graveyards as there are sloshing from one gambling hall to another.

Doc tells Red Eagle, "This is where the money is, and it's the perfect place to stage our first train wreck. Let's get ready and bring the caboose to the center of town."

After Red Eagle pulls the train into town, Doc gets out and stands in the back of the caboose. Addressing a hundred crusty miners, thugs, and cutthroats who hang around towns where a

Fort Worth & Denver Line wreck 1918 – U. S. Library of Congress

railroad terminates, he says, "We're going to stage a train crash in Denver. You can be witness to this once-in-a-lifetime opportunity. This sensational train wreck will draw the miners from Colorado and city slickers from Saint Louis. The bars, billiard rooms, and gambling halls will boom as never before."

Doc clears his throat. "Who here has ever seen a train wreck?" The miners stand around murmuring to themselves. "I'll ask y'all again: have any of ya ever in your life seen a train wreck?"

"Who the heck are you?" one of the miner's asks, his face red and angry.

Doc launches into his pitch. "The name's Doc Leonard, my good man, and I've been wrecking trains all across the Western territories. Almost got killed a few times doing it too, and lived to tell the tale! And now I've come here to offer you the most exciting offer this town has ever seen. An offer *so grand*, you can't turn it down. You, yes, and you"—Doc points to two of the men—"can be witness to this once-in-a-lifetime opportunity. This sensational event will draw people from all across the great state of Colorado to this town."

A miner asks, "What's in it for us?" Other miners shout at Doc, wanting to know the same.

Doc tries to calm the crowd. "I can assure you, my gold-digging friends, that this event will make business boom. Everyone will be drinking from your saloons, buying food from your diners, and gambling in your halls."

The miners continue murmuring, and one miner steps out of the crowd. "Credit and goodwill have not yet made it to Denver!" he shouts. "We need a guarantee that we will make money."

Doc's booming voice carries on the wind. He foolishly tells the men, "If every one of you don't make money on the events, you can hang me from the tallest tree in Denver!" Doc has struck a chord with the miners, and they clap their hands and cheer.

Doc and Red Eagle begin setting up their train crash in the summertime. Doc drives the locomotives up and down the Colorado rails, pulling a string of old passenger cars plastered with gaudy posters advertising the event. The miners have posters outside their doors and signs welcoming out-of-towners.

Red Eagle jumps from the locomotive advertising the event and walks into the caboose that has been transformed into an office.

Doc looks up from the piles of money he is counting. "The entire territory knows about the train crash. Children are lining the tracks in the morning when I pass. Parents come out and tell me that they'll all be there for the big event. This is the biggest event ever to come to Denver."

CHAPTER 14

At the railway station in Yuma, Arizona, the late trains from Colorado have arrived with hordes of people aboard. Over thirty thousand thrill-seekers pour into the makeshift community perched against the mountains. There is a virtual tent city set up with bars, restaurants, latrines, and an open-air market. Business is booming, but everyone's becoming impatient for the train crash. The entire territory knows about it and has come to watch the biggest event ever. Children are lining the tracks and playing, while their parents are talking and setting up tents.

The next day, Red Eagle goes to the caboose to talk to Doc again. Doc is still sitting in the corner counting piles of money. "Doc?" Red Eagle says, but Doc doesn't look up. He continues to flip through his money.

Finally, Doc says, "Would you look at this, Injun? Been using the railroad's telegraph to fill the newspapers with this headline." Doc holds the newspaper clipping up. "It says 'the duel of the iron monsters'! Wha'd'ya think, huh? Pretty catchy?" Red Eagle just nods.

Doc continues to count money and says, "I got two more miles of track laid out. This is great business, Injun. Our enterprise is booming! Better get this show on the road tomorrow. These folks are getting all riled up and drunk as skunks! And to think I have to stay sober to drive the train!" He stops sorting money for a moment and looks at Red Eagle. "How are you doing with your reading lessons?"

Red Eagle juts his chin out proudly. "I am learning to write my ABC's. Rachael got me some books on writing. Thanks for asking, Doc."

Doc smiles and stares out the window. He is really proud of Red Eagle and can't believe how far he's come from the days when they had their wagon.

"Some of the people have rigged a tank car and filled it with whiskey, with nozzles attached like a giant keg," Red Eagle tells him with a smile. Doc starts to run outside, but Red holds him back, pointing at paperwork that needs to be filled out. "Let them have their fun. And we need to go over the plans of how the wreck will take place."

They hear someone knocking on the door to the caboose. Doc says, "Come on in!" The town constable of Denver walks in. "Greetings, Doc. I'm the town constable. Some of the miners have brought a railroad tank car and filled it with whiskey."

"Can we get in on that action?" Doc asks, and the constable is clearly not amused.

"They've built a makeshift bar around it and attached fifty nozzles to the car. The whole town is walking around in a drunken stupor. You'd better get this show on the road before we have a riot."

"Thanks, Constable." Doc turns and tells Red Eagle, "Let's get the last of the track laid down for the train crash."

"I'll have the site completed later tomorrow," says Red Eagle.

"Then we'll plan for the crash tomorrow," the constable says as he turns to leave.

"Tomorrow is the day," Doc says with a huge smile.

The next day, Doc and Red Eagle make final preparations for the head-on collision. They walk the rails on the outskirts of town. The selected site is just beyond the rambling tents and whiskey tank car. "Good job, Red," says Doc. "This is the perfect site for the train crash."

"Straight, flat area. Easy for people to see the crash."

"Finish the tracks, and let's have a crash."

Doc tells the foreman, "Let's get going on this. We need the final rails of track put together immediately. I want the collision point to be just past the whiskey tank car. That will be the halfway point."

"Whatever you say. You're paying for this."

Doc tells his men to get the tracks assembled immediately. Fifty men begin setting spikes with sledgehammers. Later that day, the men complete the final preparations along the two miles of old track.

The latest trains from the Colorado and Western Line trains and the Union Pacific Railroad arrive in Denver with hordes of people aboard. Doc sees the prosperity that he has brought, not only to himself but to every town where they will hold their event. "This is a great business, Red Eagle," he says. "The Western and Colorado lines and Union Pacific are paying us three dollars for each rider that rides on their shuttle."

Red Eagle knows that they had better not fail. "We had better give them a great show, 'cause these folks are getting restless."

Rachael knocks on the door of the caboose. She doesn't wait for an answer but walks straight in. She has Doc's full attention. "Partner, you haven't even let me know what is going on here. I just heard from other people that the crash is tomorrow."

Doc stops what he's doing and thinks about what Rachael has said for a moment. "Miss Weatherford, I'd like to take you on a tour of the crash site." She smiles. "I'd love to."

This will be his finest hour in showmanship. Rachael is disarmingly friendly and clings to Doc's arm. She is staring up at Doc in childlike awe. It is obvious to everyone that Rachael enjoys being part of the excitement.

Doc is a little excited to have the attention of this young filly. "Hop on my horse, and we'll tour the site," he says. Rachael and Doc exit the train and ride to the site along the two miles of rail on Doc's horse. Doc stops his horse for a moment and looks back at her. "What do you think, Rachael? How do you feel about being part of all this?"

"I wouldn't know. When I was younger, I was in and out of courthouses with my dad. We were gypsies. He'd always be getting locked up for something like trespassing or vagrancy. He started to read about the law and started to get pretty good with his law books and helping other gypsies. He became a jailhouse lawyer. People were always trying to run us out of town. We were never part of anything. Then my dad would speak about constitutional rights—freedom of religion, freedom of speech. Only when we had our freedom would we know what it was like to be free."

"Well, now, partner, in this road show you've got to know as much about trains as you do about freedom of speech. Where would you fit in?" Doc says, teasing her.

Rachael launches into an anything-you-can-do-I-can-do routine, and she jumps into the cab of the idle locomotive. "See here, Doc. When controls are set, the pressure gauges and boiler are operational. All levers and controls indicate that the engine is ready to run."

"But there ain't no fire in the boiler, and how about the barometer?" he says with a grin.

Rachael can't be tricked that easily. "You can't fool me, Doc. You don't have barometers on trains. As for the boilers ..."

Undaunted and grunting, Rachael tosses her hat and coat onto the bench and begins to stoke the furnace. She is dripping wet with sweat.

Rachael shovels lumps of coal the size of a man's head. She finally starts to wear down. Her red curls are dripping wet, and her hair looks like copper stalactites.

With an unladylike grunt, she heaves a shovelful of coal toward the boiler door. It misses its mark, bounces off the furnace, and lands on her pretty high-top shoes. "Ouch!" She turns around again and bends down to shovel more coal. Doc laughs as he leans against the cab. Then he tries to make a pass at Rachael by grabbing her bottom.

Rachael turns around with the shovel in her hand and swings it at Doc, just barely missing his head. "Don't ever do that again."

Doc chuckles and says, "Miss Weatherford, you're doing it all wrong. I was just trying to help."

Just then, Red Eagle walks in. "What are you doing, Doc?"

Doc gestures with his head toward the door. "Get out of here, Red. This is none of your business."

Red Eagle says, "I take care of Rachael." Doc takes a swing at Red Eagle, and his punch lands solidly on Red Eagle's jaw. Red doesn't flinch. Doc throws all his weight into another punch to Red's stomach. Red Eagle still doesn't move and asks Doc, "Have you had enough?"

Rachael grabs her coat and hat and steps toward the door. Doc laughs. "I was just joking, Red."

"Ha, real funny," Red Eagle says.

Rachael is upset with Doc. She is upset with herself for thinking for a moment that she could actually like Doc. "That was not funny, Doc. Don't ever touch me again."

CHAPTER 15

DENVER, AUGUST 1891

The day of the big event has arrived. Doc's idea has mushroomed into a freewheeling, free-spending circus. The two hillsides surrounding the collision point are packed with thousands of people standing shoulder to shoulder. Every foot of space is occupied. Some people stand on wagon beds. Others climb trees and the water tower for a vantage point. Curtain time is near.

United States Federal Marshal Bradshaw and Thomas O'Reily work their way through the crowd toward Doc's office. They are both clean-cut, rugged, and carrying sidearms.

Agent Bradshaw flashes his badge to one of the onlookers. "Federal Marshal Bradshaw. Can you tell me where Doc Leonard is?"

A man in the crowd shouts, "He's over there in the caboose."

The marshal and O'Reily enter the caboose without knocking. Marshal Bradshaw identifies himself and flashes his badge.

Thomas O'Reily does not go unnoticed by Rachael. He is a well-dressed, handsome gunslinger in his twenties and is definitely a ladies' man with an appealing smile and striking charm. He has the eyes of a wild animal, an animal that observes everything and misses nothing. He's a hired gun through and through—and most certainly hired by the railroad.

Tom speaks to Rachael. "Excuse me, miss. I'm Tom O'Reily from the Railroad Safety Commission. I have an injunction from the United States Federal Court to stop the forthcoming train wreck."

"What? Just a minute," she says.

O'Reily goes over to Doc at his desk, cornering him. Bradshaw walks straight past Rachael and drops the injunction on the desk. "Are you Doc Leonard?"

"Ye-e-s?" he says suspiciously.

Bradshaw continues on. "By the authority vested in me by the United States federal government and its surrounding territories, you are hereby served with this injunction. You are to cease and desist from any further activities pertaining to the dangerous practice of staging a train crash on public lands."

Doc and Red Eagle exchange looks of panic. Bradshaw and O'Reily look stern. Thomas O'Reily carries his holster as though he's ready to start shooting. Doc starts to be a showman again and tries to think about ways to get out of this predicament.

"Mr. Bradshaw, Mr. O'Reily, do you fully understand the magnitude of this spectacular event? Do you completely and totally grasp what it is we have scheduled to perform here today? And for you and this great nation to deem it unsafe or dangerous—why, it's only wrecking two trains for the purpose of entertainment. And mind you, these trains are located a very safe distance from the crowd! Now, all I ask is that you witness today's event, and if you are still compelled to serve me this injunction, then I solemnly swear never to wreck a train again. However, in less than an hour, you and thirty thousand other spectators can claim to have seen this dazzling opportunity, up close and personal ... and for you, free of charge. Now, wha'd'ya say to accepting this generous offer?"

Tom replies, "What if we say no?"

Bradshaw smiles. "Then I could just take you to jail."

Doc pleads a bit, trying to talk his way out of this situation. "Can't you just report back to the federal government in Washington that you got here too late?"

Bradshaw smirks. "Nice try, but we've got our orders."

Thomas O'Reily is obviously the one in control. He looks at the desk and sees the mountain of cash. He has an idea.

He says, "Agent Bradshaw, could you please wait outside and secure the site?"

The lawman is a bit stunned, but he tips his hat to Rachael as he leaves. Tom rests his foot on the bunk bed. "I've got another idea, Doc."

Tom O'Reily eyes Doc and then Red Eagle and Rachael. He looks around the shabby caboose.

Doc sees Tom eyeing the cashbox. "We've got ninety thousand dollars already in this cashbox, all of it from legitimate railroad fares."

Tom leans close to Doc and whispers, "Let me see if I've got this straight, the two of you—"

Rachael interjects, "The three of us."

Tom says, "The three of you are staging a train wreck in this hole-in-the-wall called Denver, and you're going to walk away with ninety thousand?"

Doc is pleased with himself. "That's right. And this is just the start. We'll get three times this many people in bigger towns." Doc looks at Tom very seriously. "This is the chance of a lifetime. Isn't there anything you can do?"

There is a long silence. Tom stares at the floor and finally looks up at Doc with a grin. "Well, why don't you just call me partner?" Doc and Rachael rush forward to grasp Tom's hand. "You can call me Tom. And I want one fourth of the action from here on in."

Doc says, "Here we go again."

"Let me repeat: we're all partners," Tom says.

"Okay, I get the point. Done," Doc tells him.

"Well, partner, you know anything about trains?" asks Red Eagle.

"I'm from the Railroad Safety Commission. And when the railroad hires someone, they make certain that we know all about trains, inside and out."

"Good. You're going to drive one of the trains in the wreck!" Red Eagle says, grinning.

Tom is about to protest, but somehow the look in Rachael's eyes changes his mind. Red Eagle catches the look; Doc is too overjoyed to notice it.

Special Agent Thomas O'Reily leaves the caboose and goes to speak with Agent Bradshaw. "The event is going to go on as planned," says Tom. "The judge of the US Federal Court forgot to sign the injunction."

Bradshaw can't believe it. "My God, I thought they wouldn't notice. So they're going ahead with the crash?"

Tom seems unconcerned now and says, "As planned."

CHAPTER 16

The impatient crowd chants for the festivities to begin. Many have been waiting for over a week to see the crash.

The crowd cannot see the two locomotives, for they rest a half mile apart at opposite ends of the single track. Doc, riding Damit, his magnificent white-and-black horse, rides along the tracks.

Wolfe Londoner, the first mayor of Denver, Colorado, stands on a platform in front of the crowd and says, "Thank you all for being here today and for visiting our town. I know that many of you have traveled great distances to be here today. We hope that you enjoy your visit and consider staying in our beautiful city a while longer. But you aren't here to hear me speak all day, so without further delay, enjoy the show and let the festivities begin."

A fireworks flare is sent skyward, signaling the two locomotives to begin their forward charge.

Doc drops the hat to signal the beginning of the charge. Tom pulls the throttle wide open and lashes down the whistle chord. His locomotive lurches forward and begins pounding down the track.

In the other train, Red Eagle goes through the same motions, but his engine is locked in the reverse position. He struggles with the controls in the train cabin but without success. Red Eagle says, "Oh, no." The switcher lever for forward and reverse is still stuck in reverse.

Red Eagle's locomotive belches smoke and cinders and charges backward toward the end of the section, blocked only by a few timbers. The locomotive flies off the end of the tracks.

At the designated collision point, Tom leaps from his cab as planned. He watches his train roar past the startled crowd. Tom looks up after his jump. "What the hell?"

He and Doc and the gathered thousands watch openmouthed as the lone engine races in from one side of the arena and out the other side. There is a tremendous explosion, but the crash is witnessed by absolutely no one. A gray cloud of smoke rises on the horizon. Some stand and watch the puff of smoke, shocked into silence, and others begin to shout.

A man in the crowd starts shouting that they should lynch Doc. "Let's get him! Get Doc!" The fun-loving crowd becomes an angry mob. Another man shouts out, "He said we could hang him. Well, let's do it."

Tom runs to Rachael. "Quickly, grab all the money and meet me and Red Eagle at the station platform. You'd better grab Doc's horse too in case we need to get away quickly."

The angry mob chases Doc to the caboose. Doc rushes in and barricades the door. He is frustrated and in disbelief at his change of fortune. "I can't believe this," he says to himself. "Everything was planned so well."

Hundreds of angry miners and roughnecks brandish guns and begin to shoot at the caboose. Doc hits the floor as glass and splintered clapboard shatter around him.

Tom mounts the steps of the caboose and signals to the crowd. "Now hold on." A bottle goes flying at Tom's head. He ducks just in time and fires his shotgun into the air.

"By order of the United States federal government, this is an illegal gathering!"

Tom fires another shot in the air and waits for the crowd to calm down. "I have an injunction." Tom pulls the injunction from his coat pocket. "And I have a warrant for the arrest of Doc Leonard. He's going to get what's coming to him! He's going to hang!"

The crowd cheers in agreement. He flashes his railroad inspector's badge. "I'm a federal marshal. I'm going in after Doc. This charlatan will receive his justice!"

A man in the crowd shouts, "We want to hang him!" The crowd cheers.

Tom is excited with the anticipation of future violence. "And hang he will!" Tom kicks through the door and slams it behind him. "Doc, come on out."

Doc is hiding in the corner and snarls at Tom. "Some partner you turned out to be. I knew I couldn't trust you. Now you're going to hang me?"

Tom replies, "Shut up, Doc. We haven't got much time."

CHAPTER 17

Minutes pass, and the crowd becomes noisy again. The door to the caboose opens, and Doc exits. His hands are tied behind his back, and Tom pushes him forward. At the sight of Doc, the restless crowd cheers again. "We want him to hang!"

Tom drags Doc out of the caboose. Tom shouts, "And hang he will! You're all going to get your money's worth today! Let's get this varmint to the hanging tree."

The crowd can smell blood. At the hanging tree just outside of town, they are near where the train crash was supposed to take place. A noose is placed around Doc's neck. Doc is standing on a packing crate, and Tom is about to kick it over. The crowd is going crazy.

T.P. & W.R (Toledo, Peoria & Western Railroad) train wreck August 10, 1887. Over 250 killed and wounded. Ten coaches piled in a space of 40 x 100 feet - U.S. Library of Congress

Tom tells Doc, "By the powers vested in me as a federal agent of the United States government, you are found guilty of willful violation of this federal injunction, perjury, incitement to riot, and treason."

Tom moves closer to Doc and whispers in his ear, "Remember—kick your legs and stick out your tongue.

Oh, I almost forgot: when you've stopped kicking, you've got to wet your pants."

Doc gives Tom a wide stare. "What!"

Tom continues to whisper, "Doc, if you want this performance to go over, you have got to wet your pants." Tom says loudly so the crowd can hear, "Any last words, Doc Leonard?"

Doc stares at Tom and shouts, "Go to hell, all of you!"

Tom steps down from the crate and, without any warning, suddenly kicks it out from under Doc's feet. The crowd cheers as Doc's legs kick and scramble.

Many in the crowd turn away in disgust as Doc's legs stop kicking, his tongue sticks out, and a stream of liquid trickles from his boot.

An hour later, Doc's body is loaded into a packing crate and put aboard a Union Pacific train departing from Denver to Saint Louis.

Tom tells the porter, "Place the coffin in the freight car. I have to take the body back to Washington, DC."

Red Eagle helps Tom and the porter pull the packing crate carrying Doc's body inside the empty freight car. Rachael goes with Damit into the freight car.

The porter says, "Heard the guy got what was coming to him."

Tom replies, "Justice was served."

Once inside the freight car, Tom slides the door shut. He says, "Rachael, light the lantern."

Rachael lights the kerosene lantern, and the boxcar lights up with flickering light. Everyone's expression is very sad and concerned. Tom doesn't seem to notice or care. He pries the top off the crate, and everyone looks inside. Doc's twisted body lies stuffed in the crate, his face distorted, his tongue gruesomely hanging out of the corner of his mouth. Doc then opens one eye and flashes a smile. Rachael screams loudly, and Red stumbles backward a bit.

Doc is beaming. "Well, how was I?"

Tom laughs. "Finest performance I ever saw. Almost brought a tear to my eye."

Red Eagle helps Doc out of the crate. Rachael only glares at him, still too shocked for words.

Tom exclaims, "I guess you're all wondering how I did it?"

Rachael is shocked and embarrassed. "That was a fine performance, Doc. Okay, how did you do it?"

Tom tells the group, "Well, I fashioned a neck brace out of old cable. Cushioned supports were made from the bed upholstery and placed under Doc's armpits to hold his weight."

As Tom is telling the story, Doc rubs his neck where the cable dug into his flesh. In a hoarse voice, he says, "Where'd you ever learn that trick?"

"Read about it in one of those Western novels."

Doc jumps up abruptly, horrified. "You mean you never tried it before?"

Tom smiles at him. "There has to be a first time for everything. That's showmanship!"

Rachael is upset now. "That was a mean trick, Tom."

"What do you mean? If I didn't jimmy-rig something quick, Doc would be dead."

Rachael crosses her arms across her chest. "You could have at least told us that Doc was alive. All of us were upset, and for no reason."

Tom still doesn't get it. "That would have ruined the surprise," he says.

"I can't believe that you'd never done that before!" Doc says. "I was being used as a guinea pig!"

Tom is really surprised at everyone's lack of gratitude. "You would think that somebody would at least say thanks for saving your worthless life."

Red Eagle clears his throat. "Thank you, Tom."

"Yeah, thanks, Tom, for saving Doc and giving us time to get out of there," Rachael says.

Doc looks at Tom with a bit of suspicion and replies, "Well, then, thanks, Tom. Been a long time since I pissed in my own pants."

"Don't mention it." Tom claps a hand on Doc's shoulder. They all start laughing, realizing that the outcome was fine.

Doc asks, "Where's this train heading?"

Tom replies, "Going east to bury you."

"I can't go east. I've got to go to California."

"Too late for that, Doc. Maybe another day."

Doc asks, "Where's all the money."

"What money?" Tom says, shrugging.

"You know what I'm talking about. The money."

Tom laughs. "You're supposed to be dead. Now you want money? You're sounding kind of ungrateful."

Doc's face grows red. "We're partners."

"Don't worry, Doc," says Rachael. "As we were leaving, Tom and I grabbed the money. I'm going to take the money you borrowed from the gypsy's and send it back to my father at the next stop. I also managed to get Damit."

"Thanks, partners," Doc says.

CHAPTER 18

THE HOLDUP, OCTOBER 12, 1892

The quartet is bound for Kansas City next, traveling in a crowded passenger car. Half the occupants are asleep, while the others stare out at the endless prairie moving by. Doc is sound asleep in his seat. His neck still bears the marks from the hanging.

Rachael and Red Eagle are sitting together, and she is patiently working with him, teaching him to read. He reads Edgar Allan Poe's "Eldorado."

> Gaily bedight,
> A gallant knight,
> In sunshine and in shadow,
> Had journeyed long,
> Singing a song,
> In search of Eldorado.
>
> But he grew old—
> This knight so bold—
> And o'er his heart a shadow—
> Fell as he found
> No spot of ground
> That looked like Eldorado.

And, as his strength
Failed him at length,
He met a pilgrim shadow—
"Shadow," said he,
"Where can it be—
This land of Eldorado?"

"Over the Mountains
Of the Moon,
Down the Valley of the Shadow,
Ride, boldly ride,"
The shade replied—
"If you seek for Eldorado!"

Rachael is beaming at him when he finishes. "That was great. You're really getting the hang of this."

"Thanks, Rachael. You great teacher. What is 'Eldorado'?"

"In the poem, Eldorado means that they are all on a quest."

"That is like us! We are looking for Eldorado."

"I believe that we all are looking for Eldorado. Sometimes you never know what you are really looking for."

"The trick must be to decide what to search for. There are so many paths. What do you search for, Rachael?"

"At first, all I wanted was to get the money returned. Now, I want to be famous."

"Why do you want to be famous?"

"So that I don't just vanish from life without anyone remembering me."

"I don't know what I want, since the Spirit in the sky hasn't revealed it to me yet. Sometimes I think Eldorado is right in front of me but I can't see it."

Red Eagle decides to take a break from reading to share a pint of the "medicine" with Tom and discuss the staged train wrecks in their future.

He stops for a moment to see if he can read the wanted posters hanging inside the train. One reads, "The Doolin-Dalton Gang, Also

Known as the Wild Bunch, Wanted Dead or Alive $5,000 Reward." It has a picture of the gang. Red Eagle is proud of himself for learning to read so quickly. With a huge grin on his face, he goes to find Tom.

After a few drinks, Red Eagle is slurring his words and becoming more incoherent with each gulp of whiskey. "What are you looking for, Tom? What is your Eldorado?"

Tom says, "You are becoming a philosopher. Actually, Red, I don't know what I'm here for."

"Let me know when you find out."

"What are you going to do, Red?"

"We're gonna stage an even bigger train wreck. The biggest eeeeverrr."

Tom laughs. "Maybe the engine won't get stuck in reverse?"

Red Eagle laughs with him. "No stuck engine! Yeah."

"Don't worry. It wasn't your fault. Anyway, I'll be back. I'm going to stretch my legs."

Tom walks, a bit wobbly, down the aisle.

Red Eagle continues to mumble to himself about the rail disasters. "I'm gonna wreck the train good."

His claim startles two old women seated directly in front of him. The women exchange astonished looks and crane their necks in order to hear more.

"No, I'll ... I'll derail, gonna derail it. Dee-rail. Gonna derail the white man's iron horse. Eldorado!"

The two old ladies panic. They can't believe their ears. Tom walks down the aisle past the women. One of them pulls at Tom's coat and speaks in a panicked, hushed tone. "Sir, that savage Injun behind us says he's going to wreck this train."

Tom glances at Red Eagle. His eyes are closed, and he's resting in his seat. Tom sarcastically says, "Yes, ma'am, he does look really dangerous," and he walks away.

"Aren't you going to do anything?" she asks, her voice shrill.

"Oh, no, ma'am, not me. I'm the biggest coward in the world when it comes to Injuns, especially sleeping ones."

The braver of the two old ladies can't stand it any longer. She grabs her parasol, stands up, and smashes Red Eagle on the crown of his head, caving in his hat. "Wake up, Injun!" Incredibly, Red Eagle doesn't budge. He just rolls over on his side. She flogs the daylights out of Red Eagle, and the train suddenly comes to an abrupt halt.

The two doors burst open, and a masked man comes roaring in with his gun drawn, fires into the air, and yells out to the train passengers. "Stay in your seats, do as you're told, and no one will get hurt."

One of the old ladies looks up at the Doolin-Dalton Gang wanted poster and sees that the shouting gunman is Emmett—the youngest member at twenty years old. "It's the Dalton Gang," she screams.

Twenty-two-year-old Dalton Gang member Grat barrels into the train car. He tells everyone to shut up and sit down. "Get out your money and jewelry now, and put it in this bag as we walk down the aisle."

Several women scream out. Others make feeble attempts to ditch valuables under their seats. Tom is standing in the aisle, facing two of the gunmen. Rachael is awake now and quickly figures out what's going on. The other two gunmen are at Tom's back.

Emmett snarls at Tom. "You, pretty boy. You need to sit down!"

Tom gives a backward glance at the two gunmen behind him. He then looks straight ahead at the bandit giving the orders.

Tom is a little cocky and tries to take charge. "Don't want to sit down. Been sitting down the last two hundred miles," he calls out. A gunman aims his Remington .38 at Tom.

Emmett says, "All right, then. Now you can lie down for good!"

With lightning quickness, Tom is on the floor. His pistol is drawn and firing. The first two shots from his gun smash through Emmett's and Grat's hearts. Then he fires into the Pullman door behind them. Tom then whirls around and fires another shot at Frank, hitting him in the shoulder. Frank slumps to the floor dying.

Another member, Bob, enters the car and aims his shotgun at Tom. Again, Tom spins in a seated position and fires, his bullet smashing into Bob's forehead.

Frank has managed to get up and grab one of the old ladies. He stands behind her with his arm around her throat and a gun to her head, his eyes wild. Tom races to the doors of the car. "Hold on there, partner. She hasn't done nothing to ya."

Frank ducks his head behind the old lady, using her as a shield. He turns the gun, pointing toward Tom. "You're right, she hasn't done nothing to nobody. *You* are going to pay."

In the blink of an eye, Tom raises his gun and shoots Frank. Frank falls dramatically to the floor, gasping for breath, covered in blood. Tom casually kicks the man's gun away and strolls back through the car to be certain that everyone is out of danger.

Rachael has been watching in total shock at how brutally Tom killed the four Doolin-Dalton Gang members without any hesitation.

Tom announces to everyone in the train car, "Everything's okay, folks. Just an attempted holdup."

All eyes are on the handsome young Tom. Doc and Rachael stare at him as he casually reloads his revolver. All mouths and eyes are wide open. The train begins to move again.

After Tom takes his seat again, Doc jumps into the seat opposite him. "Don't tell me you got *that* from a Western novel," he says.

Tom smiles. "When the Railroad Safety Commission hires an agent, they can afford the best."

Doc and Rachael have no doubt that Thomas O'Reily is a professional hired gun and killer, employed by the railroads to discourage looting.

Doc looks around the coach. "Everybody here okay?" Instinctively, everyone just nods and sighs in relief. The old lady who was held hostage replies, "Yeah!"

Turning back to Tom, Doc says, "Looks like you have earned some reward money."

"Just happy that no one was injured."

Red Eagle, who has slept through the entire incident, wakes up and moans, "My head hurts like thunder."

CHAPTER 19

TRAIN WRECKS, 1893

The group has been on the road for a couple of years and has become well-known across the country. The four trainwreckers' exploits have taken them all over the country as they travel in style in one large, plush Pullman. They have staged train wrecks in Joplin, Missouri; Cheyenne, Wyoming; Waco, Texas; Topeka, Kansas; and Des Moines, Iowa. Crowds gather and cheer at the sight of the trains being rear-ended, sideswiped, and crashed into barns.

The trainwreckers have become celebrities in their own right. Rachael appears on the covers of newspapers next to the wrecked trains. Whenever they come into town, people line up for her autograph, and newspapermen ask for an interview.

Even with all the fame, Rachael misses her family and decides to write a letter to her father.

> Dear Father, I pray that this letter finds you well. You were correct when you said that Red Eagle should be able to protect and watch over me. He has been a faithful friend. I have taught him to read, and he's extremely intelligent.

We caught up with Doc, and he went to jail. Instead of leaving him in jail and having the money returned, we invested the ministry's money. The venture went well. I am enclosing those funds that Doc borrowed plus interest.

Red Eagle is watching me like a hawk and is keeping me safe from the vulgarities of the road. Please write to me, Papa. I pray that you and the ministry are all well.

With love from your daughter, Rachael.

Rachael's father, Luther, writes back.

Dear Rachael, thank you for the money. I hope that you are well and safe. I have seen your picture in the papers amid the carnage of wrecked locomotives. Please thank the noble savage Red Eagle for keeping you safe. Enjoy your adventure and stay safe. Godspeed, your father.

CHAPTER 20

The four trainwreckers' Pullman cruises along the tracks with Doc at the helm. He asks Tom to put more coal into the boilers.

"Doc, I've been shoveling for the last two hours," Tom says, wiping his brow.

"I take over," Red Eagle says.

"Thanks, Red Eagle," Tom says and then grabs some water and drinks down a big gulp. He pours the rest over his head to get the black coal dust off his face and goes to sit next to Rachael.

"How are you holding up with all the crashes?" he asks.

"I'm fine. I had no idea that we would be doing it for this long. I'm missing my family."

Tom nods. "When I was a kid, I was always moving. Now, I'm still moving. My father was a trainman. We'd see him one or two days a month, and then he'd be gone again. We got used to him not being there for us."

"Funny, I had the opposite. I've been used to my father always being there. I started to resent it. But now I realize how lucky I am, since you, Red Eagle, and Doc never had your fathers around."

"You are a smart young woman, Rachael Weatherford, to recognize that."

Rachael smiles at him. "I've enjoyed all of us traveling together. I am beginning to find myself."

"I'm beginning to understand myself better, and sometimes it scares me."

"Don't be scared, Tom. God must have put you here for a special reason."

"I don't know my special purpose yet," replies Tom, shrugging.

"My father always said that we'd never know the reason. But I keep on searching."

"I'll keep searching too. Hey, what's with you and Red Eagle?"

"Nothing. Just teaching him to read. He's really smart, Tom. I have taught hundreds of kids to read, but I'd say that Red Eagle is my best student."

"Seems like we all underestimated him. He's a really good man, even though he's still an Indian."

Rachael turns away from him, and they sit in silence for a while.

The silence is broken when Doc makes an announcement. "Prepare to disembark. We're now in Kansas City, folks."

The whistle of the locomotive can be heard inside the luxurious Pullman, which has become their new office and has a new desk made of mahogany wood. The same briefcase filled with money sits on the desk along with various papers that need to be signed or dealt with.

CHAPTER 21

Rachael enters the luxurious private car now resting on a siding on the outskirts of Kansas City. The new office was her own design, and she was responsible for the renovation of the Pullman that attracts attention wherever they go. She updated the car using Venetian baroque design, with gold-embroidered drapes, fixtures, crystal chandeliers, and velvet cushions. Even wealthy railroad barons stare at the opulent coach with envy when they see it.

Doc and Tom are seated at the desk, closing a deal with one of the local lawmen regarding the gambling operations that always manage to flourish near the staged collisions.

The sheriff says, "Our normal cut is fifty percent of the gambling operations."

"Well, now, that is a bit steep," Doc says.

"Fifty percent. Fifty percent, straight down the middle, Sheriff?" Tom says.

The sheriff thinks for a moment. There isn't much else going on around these parts. This will be the event of the decade. "Well, I suppose, since you bring those crowds with ya, there will be more than enough to go around. We could do it for twenty-five percent."

Doc leads the sheriff back out of the coach. They have gotten pretty experienced in these negotiations. It seems that everyone has their hands out.

"Glad you see it our way, Sheriff. Now, you ask any of those other towns. They appreciate our business there."

As the sheriff is leaving, Rachael brushes past him with a heavy box. She drops the box on the table with a loud thud, and Doc looks down at it. "What did the cat drag in today?" he says.

U.S. Library of Congress

Rachael smiles coyly. "Money."

There is a moment that passes quickly between them as Rachael fumbles with the box. Tom gives Doc a bit of an evil eye and then opens the box and stares into it. It is filled with shiny new engine bolts of blue steel, fresh from a local foundry. Doc and Tom exchange puzzled looks.

Doc is confused. "Darling, money in this here country is made on *paper*," he says.

Red Eagle is curled up on the velvet sofa, wearing a new pair of spectacles, and he looks rather distinguished. He is reading *Tom Sawyer* and looks up from his book to see what's going on. "Maybe she just made the money."

Rachael reaches into the box and produces a small can of grease mixed with dirt. She smears it on two of the engine bolts and plops one of the grimy chunks of steel in Doc's hand, the other in Tom's. They exchange another look.

With a smug look of superiority, Rachael produces a small, hand-lettered card and hands it to Doc. Doc reads slowly, "Genuine souvenirs from demolished locomotives. One dollar each."

Rachael is really proud of herself. "You know the way thousands of people comb through each wreck, looking for a keepsake to take away with them? Well, step right up and get them, folks. Each one gen-u-ine and only one dollar!"

Doc shakes his head at Rachael's ingenuity. "You're a genius! Damn clever."

The two look at each other again, something passing between them. She catches Tom staring at her, and she clears her throat and continues on with the second part of her idea. Red is now sitting up on the sofa, listening intently.

"That's not all. I had another idea! Each train pulls three or four old wooden coaches, just the way we always do. But here's the real crowd-pleaser. Before the trains start, we soak the inside of each coach with kerosene. We then add several buckets of red-hot coals in the aisles. On impact"—she claps her hands together loudly—"the buckets tip over, and boom! The cars burst into flames. A train wreck and the Fourth of July, all in one!"

Doc is speechless. "You sure you never wrecked trains before this?"

"Doc, you're the originator. I'm just the student," she answers, gleeful.

"You've changed, Rachael. I think it's a great idea," he says. "When we began, we were going to do one train crash. We've all made enough money not to work for a long time. I am going to head out to California pretty soon and set down some roots."

Rachael is not ready to quit. "I can't believe I'm hearing this from you. I thought you enjoyed the excitement."

Doc knows when it's time to quit. He is ready to follow his dreams. "I've enjoyed our business. As all of you know, I always intended to go to the West. I'm stuck here. There is nothing more for me here."

"I love this business," says Rachael. "I was stuck in a gypsy camp before this. Doc, don't do it. There is nothing else for me. I always dreamed of being on the road, but this is better than I ever imagined."

Doc says, "Rachael, you are beautiful, famous, and smart. You can do anything you want in the future."

But Rachael knows that this is it for her. She can't do anything else. "I can't go back," she says. "What else could I do?"

Doc thinks for a moment. "I can't answer that. A man can only answer to his maker. You're going to have to figure that out on your own."

"I need to get out of here," Tom says. "Come on, Rachael. Let's take a walk."

Rachael can't understand how everything has gone wrong. "I thought it was such a great idea," she says.

Red Eagle knows this is just life. Everything always changes. "All of us are moving swiftly like the stars, the sun, and the moon," he says.

CHAPTER 22

As Rachael and Tom take a walk, she tells him, "Doc is getting all soft on us."

"I don't think so. He's just ready to follow a different trail."

"This was the trail that he forged. We were just riding along."

"That's the point, Rachael. At some point, you need to create your own road."

"What road are you following?" she asks.

He stops walking and turns to her. "You never noticed? You don't remember the first time I walked into the Pullman?"

"I remember you were looking at me. You had a funny look in your eyes."

"That wasn't a funny look. I thought that there could be something special between us," he says and softly puts a hand on her shoulder.

"I never knew. I just thought that you wanted a new career."

"I had a fine career."

"Why didn't you say?"

Tom shrugs. "I was afraid."

"That doesn't scare me. You're a good man."

"I've killed people. Lots of people."

"Lots? That's all behind you, Tom."

She stares at the ground for a moment, silent, and begins walking again. When he catches up to her, she says, "This is the kind of place where I would like to settle down one day."

"Me too. I've spent my whole life traveling on trains. My father was a train engineer, and we never lived in the same area for very long when I was growing up. Now I'm doing the same thing."

"This seems like a great place to raise a family," Rachael says. "I know I'm not ready for that yet. But I know I will be one day."

"I still have lots of places to see, Rachael. I don't think this is my destiny. My whole life has involved going from battle to battle. I lost my soul long ago."

"I'm sorry, Tom."

"I'm sorry too."

"Thanks for talking to me. We'd better be getting back to the train."

"Yeah, we're still on the move."

As they're walking back to the train, they pass the Ole Saloon.

Tom says, "I'm going inside to check on Doc. I'll be back in a few."

It's a ramshackle old saloon. Several horses are tied up in front, and there are two double-hinged doors to leave and enter the saloon.

Red Eagle sits outside on the wooden steps, surrounded by a group of Indian children. They listen, spellbound, as he tells them about how he wrecks the great trains.

CH & D 1897 train wreck, Dayton, Ohio 1897 – Wilbur Wright and Orville Wright photographer, U.S. Library of Congress

"Hey, Red Eagle, don't put any foolish ideas into the kids' minds," Tom says.

Red Eagle smiles at Tom and continues his story, "I smash the white man's trains. Just always remember that it is important to keep your dignity. We are eagles, and we soar. Maintain your dignity, and you will always fly."

Tom walks inside where Doc is playing poker. A few empty bottles of whiskey sit on his table, and Doc is reeling drunk. A young barmaid in her late teens or early twenties makes a move on Doc. She gazes into his eyes and nearly smothers him with her generous affections, truly taken with him. She runs her fingers through his hair and then touches his shoulder as she passes by with a tray of drinks.

"You want another round, Mister Train Man?" she asks.

"Well, now, only if you're paying, sweetheart," he answers with a wide grin and a wink. She bats her eyelashes at him, and though Doc is drunk, he's not so drunk that he doesn't know what he's doing. He stumbles as he gets up from his chair. "Honey, there's room for one more on my train," he says, his words slurred.

"Well, captain, I'm all aboard," she says, laughing at her own joke.

Doc puts his hat on her head, and she starts giggling girlishly, caressing his face and the back of his neck.

Tom walks over to Doc's table and grabs his arm lightly. "Come on now, Doc. Let's get back to the train."

Doc pulls his arm away roughly. "You're interrupting my game, which I'm *winning*," Doc says, trying to whisper but failing miserably. The barmaid giggles. Doc looks over at her and laughs, realizing she heard him. He turns back to Tom. "See? Mind your own business, *friend*."

"Come on, Doc," Tom says again.

Rachael enters the saloon and stands behind Doc and Tom with her hands on her hips, looking infuriated.

When Tom notices that Rachael is behind them, he says, "Come on, Doc. This is a really good time to leave."

"Ahem," Rachael says, attempting to get Doc's attention. She gives the barmaid a cold stare and turns back to Doc. "The supplies you ordered just arrived at the train," she says, trying to get him away from the barmaid diplomatically.

The barmaid shifts closer to Doc, but he doesn't get the hint.

He says, "I didn't order any supplies! Scat, both of you."

"Oh, yes, you did," she says, glaring at him.

Doc finally catches on. "Oh, yeah, the supplies! Right, the supplies, yeah."

He turns back to the barmaid and says, "Excuse me, honey. I have to get back to the train."

Doc staggers out of the bar, crashing into tables as he exits, and the barmaid glares at Rachael. "Wha'd'ya go and do that for?"

"Time for Mr. Leonard to get his beauty rest. Lord knows he needs it."

The barmaid crosses her arms. "I think he's old enough to take care of himself."

"Oh, don't you go worrying your pretty li'l' head off, sweetie! Doc ain't the marryin' kind."

"That's just cuz he ain't your kind, is all! He knows what he wants in a woman, and it ain't you."

Tom senses a fight coming. "Uh, been a real swell evening, ladies. Got to check on Doc! Good night!" he says, grabbing Doc's poker chips and rushing out the door after him.

Rachael is hurt by the barmaid's remarks. "Doc would certainly never be interested in the likes of you. Besides"—she pauses—"he has syphilis."

Rachael looks smugly at the barmaid, whose eyes are wide with shock, and Rachael walks out of the bar through the swinging double doors.

"What are you guys doing? I'm going back inside," Doc says.

Rachael crosses her arms. "Suit yourself."

Doc staggers back into the bar with a smile on his face. He wobbles over to the table and puts his hand on the barmaid's shoulders.

Doc smiles and winks at her again. "Hey, cutie pie, still wanna hop aboard the train? Whoo whoo!" he says, imitating a train's whistle.

The barmaid's eyes blaze, showing her disgust. "Get ya hands offa me!"

Doc tries to pull her outside. "Come on, honey. I'm gonna show you the Southern Pacific line!" he says, laughing.

"Don't ever touch me, you maniac."

He tries to grab her again. "Come on, I was only trying to have some fun."

The terrified girl grabs an empty whiskey bottle and shatters it over his head. He staggers and then falls to the floor, passing out.

Tom and Red Eagle go back into the bar to drag Doc out and get him back to the train.

Rachael is still standing outside the bar, gazing at Doc sadly when they bring him out. She sees Tom coming toward her and tries to hide her face, but he notices that it looks as though she's been crying.

"I'm going to walk back to the rail car myself," she tells him.

CHAPTER 23

Doc and Tom sit at the desk in the Pullman, talking and looking over various advertising posters for their next stunt.

Doc says, "Hmmm, I like this one, the steam boiler belching hot coals, the steam belching from the stacks, seems to have the desired effect. People hate to see violence, but we can't seem to turn our heads away when it occurs."

Red Eagle is curled up on one of the velvet-covered couches with a book on his lap.

Rachael enters with a bundle of papers under her arms. "Get ready, cuz we're all going to work for the railroad."

Doc puts down the poster. He looks confused. "Beg your pardon?"

Rachael launches into her sales pitch. "One of the railroad officials got in contact with me, and they want us to stage a crash on behalf of a presidential candidate they're backing. He's trying to get in with the Democrats, somebody named—" Rachael fumbles with the papers. "Here it is, William Jennings Bryan, 'the Great Commoner.'" Rachael passes out the papers. "He's running for president against Grover Cleveland. One of Bryan's advisers is a prominent railroad tycoon. He wants to use Doc's train wrecks to attract crowds for Bryan. He wants the maximum audience for the maximum exposure."

Doc smiles. "Sounds pretty good to me! Wha'd'ya think, Injun?"

Red Eagle opens his eyes and turns to Rachael, confused and incredulous that he would now be working for the government. "This is how elections work? People decide who is more popular?"

"That's how American politics work, chief," Doc says under his breath.

"I'm not so sure about this," says Tom. "You know, when I wired the Railroad Commission from Denver years ago that I was too late to stop the collision, I also wired my resignation. No, no, I don't like this idea. As far as I'm concerned, if there is something in it for the railroad, it's a bad idea."

Presidential Candidate William Jennings Bryan, U.S. Library of Congress

Red Eagle doesn't like it either. He says sarcastically, "As long as I get my land back," and Rachael frowns.

Doc tries reasoning with his partners. "We should at least be willing to speak with the railroad bosses and listen to their proposal."

Tom is adamant. "I refuse to have anything to do with the deal. You can do whatever you want, Doc, but don't count me in."

Doc looks at Rachael. "What about you? What do you think?"

She glares at him. "I don't know. Why don't you go and ask some other woman for an opinion?" she says.

"This is business!" he says indignantly.

Rachael huffs out of the room. Tom gets up to follow her, calling out her name. Red Eagle and Doc exchange looks. Red Eagle's look clearly says that Doc should know better, but Doc just shrugs it off.

CHAPTER 24

RAILROAD COMMISSION OFFICE, 1896

Doc and Red Eagle go to Saint Louis to meet with Bryan's representatives. They enter the plush executive office of the Illinois and Central Railroad.

Red Eagle lounges in the outer offices. He pulls out a book titled *Broken Treaties* from under his coat, puts on his glasses, and starts to read.

Doc goes to the secretary's desk and introduces himself. She tells him, "Come this way, sir. Everyone is waiting for you inside." Red Eagle gets up to follow him into the meeting room.

She tells Red Eagle, "Um, you, Indian, can stay out here." Doc looks at Red, "Stay here, Red. I'll be back in a few." Red Eagle glares at Doc and then goes back to reading.

Doc is shown into the plush boardroom where a dozen prominent railroad bosses welcome him enthusiastically. They all have big mustaches that curl up at the end. One man named Harrison greets Doc. "Come on in, Doc, m'boy. We've been expecting you!"

Everyone who has controlling interests in the railroad lines seems to be present. A man named Quincy begins the conversation. "Thank you for coming here today."

Doc tries to be affable, but he sees this whole thing as a charade. "Let's get down to business, shall we?"

"You're a man who doesn't waste much time! I like that!" Harrison says, his words dripping with fake congeniality.

Doc is confused and not sure how to respond. "Uh, yeah, thanks."

"The offer we've decided to make is a very lucrative one, Doc. You ready for this?"

"All my business has been lucrative," Doc says, iciness frosting his words. Harrison ignores his comment.

Quincy replies, "Doc, we're giving you a guarantee of two hundred thousand dollars per event, with the railroad supplying all engines, rolling stock, and manpower. We're gonna foot the bill for *all* the advertising and publicity. *All* of it! *And* we're gonna send you to the World's Fair in Nashville, Tennessee, for an exclusive record-breaking appearance!"

"You're all very generous," Doc says, saccharine sweet. "I've been checking, and it seems merely a coincidence that all of you hold controlling interests in silver mines," The bosses eye each other warily. "And if your candidate wins, you hold the cards to controlling America's financial future."

Harrison says, "Here you go again! What keen insight! It's such a pleasure to be working with such an intelligent person as yourself. And that is why our offer to you is so attracti—"

Everyone turns as Red Eagle crashes through the door. He says, "All the land. Return the land to my people."

Doc grabs the tall Indian and tries to ease him out the door. Red Eagle tries to fight him off. "Come on, Red, not now."

Security officers burst into the inner offices and attempt to grab Red Eagle. He throws the four men to the side. "Keep your hands off me."

One of the security guards grabs his gun and points it at Red Eagle. Tom barges into the room with his gun drawn. He tells the security guards, "Don't even think about it."

Red Eagle tells the railroad bosses, "All the land and all the buffalo."

Harrison says to the security personnel, "It's okay." Turning to Tom, he says, "It's nice to see you again."

"Likewise!" Tom says.

Doc interrupts the little reunion. "I apologize, gentlemen, about my partner's unfortunate behavior. I can assure you that I will discuss your proposition with my partners."

"It's all here." Red Eagle points to his book. "All your broken promises and broken treaties." Red Eagle walks out on his own, following Tom.

Doc tells Harrison, "I'll have an answer for you by tomorrow. Good day, gentlemen!"

The three men get into the waiting carriage. As the carriage drives off, Doc yells at Red Eagle, "Red Eagle! We're in the middle of a business transaction! I'm attempting to do something for all of us. You've got to put your political views aside right now."

Red Eagle's temper flares. "How can you tell me to put it aside? Were you kicked out of your home? Did you see your family suffer over and over again? Did you see your people put onto reservations?" Doc remains quiet and uncomfortable. "I can't put my political views aside. This is who I am now. I can't."

CHAPTER 25

KANSAS CITY, 1896

Tom and Rachael are in her room in the Pullman, discussing Doc's idea of leaving the train-wrecking business.

Tom says, "I think we should probably start our own business."

"I don't know, Tom. We've been together for so long."

"You heard him, Rachael. He's going to California anyway."

They hear something at her door. "What's that?" Rachael jumps up from her desk as Doc kicks the door open.

Tom says, "You're out of line, Doc." Tom is just able to get up before Doc's first punch sends him crashing into the wall.

"You backstabbers."

"We're partners, Doc," Tom says, his hands raised in front of him.

Doc tries to punch Tom again. "I'm out. We're not doing any more crashes. You two are messing with my personal life."

A brawling fistfight turns the posh Pullman into shambles. Tom sends Doc reeling backward against a wall with a flying kick and leaps for the table and draws his gun.

Doc leans against the wall, holding a hand to his bleeding mouth. "What are you going to do? Shoot me, killer."

Gasping for breath, Tom lowers his gun. Doc pulls himself up against the wall. "You're out, both of you. Get outta my sight!"

"Let's get outta here," Tom says to Rachael.

Red Eagle walks into the Pullman. "Trouble?"

Rachael storms toward Doc. "Oh, I'm out, is that it? I'm out because I want to continue with our business? And you? Are you out when you get rolled by every woman of ill repute at every railhead? You started out by stealing the ministry's money and selling fake medicine. We bailed you out and saved your life. And we're out of line?"

Rachael begins to throw all her clothes into suitcases.

"You tell your greasy railroad friends that the Bryan deal is off," Doc says, seething.

Tom puts his coat on and points a finger at Doc. "Doc, the Bryan deal is very much on. I'm staging the Bryan wreck, and I'll be in mighty good company."

Rachael says, "Come on, Red Eagle. We're leaving."

"Red Eagle stays. Doc needs friend. Looks like I'm out of a job."

"Come on, Rachael," Tom says. He puts his arm around her, and they walk out the door. Doc rushes to the platform, cursing them as they walk away.

US library of Congress

The next day, Tom and Rachael are in Forrest West's office. West is the chief organizer for the Bryan campaign and in his late forties. He is very straitlaced and represents the establishment. None of the other railroad bosses are present.

Tom is attempting to act like a showman, but his imitation is poor. "You see, here, Mr. West, our train wrecks will bring people from all over the country. We will make Doc's train wrecks sound like a one-armed man clapping in the wind by comparison."

"The railroad wishes to remain anonymous in the Bryan rally. They have already agreed to pick up the tab for all the expenses."

"Well, that's outstanding, Mr. West," Tom says, relieved. "I know you won't be disappointed."

Rachael is only half listening to the business details as she gazes out the window at the smoky Saint Louis sky. Suddenly she gasps and brings a hand to her mouth, reacting to something in the street below.

The door bursts open, and Doc enters, followed by Red Eagle. A fleeting trace of a greeting crosses Rachael's face as she sees them, but she catches herself in time.

"Gentlemen, I understand that you are in the midst of contriving some sort of exhibition involving the staged collision of two fine locomotives," Doc says.

Tom replies, "You know damned well we are."

"Mr. Leonard, you had the opportunity to show your amazing train display to the world," West says, "but you backed out too early."

"It's my game, and I can play it any way I like. And I'm afraid that this here proposed collision on behalf of Mr. William Jennings Bryan will have to be canceled."

West has seen jokers before, and Doc is definitely no exception. "Mr. Leonard, you have no jurisdiction over whether or not this performance can be canceled."

In this game of wits, Doc isn't going to be beaten by some low-level bureaucrat. "Oh, but I do!" he says. "You see, I'm the originator, founder, and inventor of the head-on train collision production." Doc takes a document out of his breast pocket. "This document bears the great seal of the Office of the Attorney General of the State of Missouri stating that, quote: 'Doc Leonard has the exclusive copyright and license to the aforementioned exhibition,' end quote."

Doc folds the papers and stuffs them back into his coat. "So you see"—Doc looks at Tom—"without my permission, you could be in a heck of a lot a trouble there, triggerman."

Tom grits his teeth. Rachael turns around and looks at West. "Can he do that?"

"Look, folks, the last thing in the world we want is to publicize a thing like this and then have the law shut us down," West says. "Our candidate, Mr. Bryan, would be terribly embarrassed." He looks at Doc. "I'm afraid that Mr. Leonard here has us over a barrel."

"Now, hold on there a minute, gentlemen," Doc says. "There is a way out of this thing, and that's my way. Let's have a William Jennings Bryan rally. Let's have us a head-on collision—the biggest, most spectacular head-on collision ever staged, an event that will have people all over the country talking about it for years."

West is bored but irritated. "I don't understand what you're talking about, Mr. Leonard."

Doc replies quickly. "I'm saying that you have my permission—on one condition." He stares straight into Rachael's puzzled eyes. "I drive one of the trains myself. Mr. Tom O'Reily drives the other train. In this crash, no one jumps." There is a deafening silence. "Think of it, gentlemen. Two men, each riding a booming iron monster, flying at each other's steam locomotive at runaway speed. The posters can read: 'The Challenge to the Death.'"

Doc turns and stares at Tom. "What's the matter, partner? Scared of a li'l' ole train wreck?"

Tom doesn't flinch. He stares intensely at Doc. "You're on!"

West is cautious and a little slower than usual. "The two of you will have to sign releases removing our candidate from any responsibility should you—"

"Get killed?" Doc says, laughing. "Don't worry, we're professionals, aren't we, Tom?" He smirks rudely at Tom. "And one more thing. I want to be certain that we get paid before the event."

West tells him, "Sure. You're not going to need the money where you're going."

Doc turns and walks out the door. Red Eagle stands at the door and shrugs his shoulders.

Tom and Rachael shake West's hand and leave the office. Tom tells her, "Doc's gone crazy. Absolutely crazy."

A group of reporters has congregated in front of Doc's Pullman, and he stops to speak with them as he returns from West's office.

A reporter asks, "We have heard that the train wreck may be called off. We'd like your comments."

"As you all know, I'm the originator of the head-on collision show. I have a document here bearing the great seal of the Office of the Attorney General of the State of Missouri stating that, quote: 'Doc Leonard has the exclusive copyright.'" The reporters groan. Doc says, "Now, hold on there a minute, gentlemen. I just returned from a meeting at the railroad offices." The reporters murmur to each other, and some complain of being fed a phony story.

"A head-on collision, the biggest ever staged."

There is a deafening silence. "Picture this: two men riding toward each other at the runaway speed and neither jumps. A challenge to the death!"

There's a mad scramble as the reporters turn and run off to get the news to the wires for their special editions.

Doc turns and walks back into the Pullman. Red Eagle stands at the door, watching the reporters, indifferent to what just happened.

Tom tells Rachael, "Doc *has* gone crazy. Sorry that it has to end like this."

"It's not over yet," she says.

CHAPTER 26

WILLIAM JENNINGS BRYAN'S RAILROAD CAR

On the observation deck atop Bryan's private railroad car, West tells Bryan, "Sir, you should take a look at this." West hands him the daily Saint Louis newspaper, which touts the headline "Challenge to the Death!"

"Let the fools go kill themselves," Bryan says. "We should distance ourselves from this lunacy."

"Frankly, sir, we don't care if both those damn fools get killed. Why, with a few well-chosen words on morality, temperance, and the Good Book, you can turn the event to your advantage. This event should draw even more spectators than ever imagined."

Bryan looks out the train window. "With this level of national publicity, we should go ahead with the railroad proposal."

William Jennings Bryan, U.S. Library of Congress

CHAPTER 27

Preparations are under way for the ultimate challenge. This is the duel of the century. Every hotel and boardinghouse in Saint Louis is filled to capacity weeks before the event. Hotels all over Saint Louis have No Vacancy signs in front of their establishments.

The rolling hills just outside Saint Louis are chosen for the site of the collision. Giant tents, makeshift foundries, and factories stand in clusters at opposite ends of a single two-mile section of track.

Doc and Red Eagle work on their giant, rolling warrior. Doc motions to Red. "Come check this out, Injun. This here's an oversized Mallet engine, designed for heavy freight service in the Rockies."

They stand next to the massive drive wheels and survey their gladiator. Doc smiles. "Ain't she beautiful? Gotta give her a name."

Red Eagle looks worried. He points to the boilers. "Boss, the boilers. What if they explode?"

Doc takes his partner's concern seriously. "Good thinking there, Injun." He tells the welders to fasten a shell of four-inch armor plate around the locomotive boiler.

William Jennings Bryan with the Sioux
Indians, U.S. Library of Congress

Tom and Rachael are with West and his group of locomotive experts. Tom mulls over what to get. "I'll need something really heavy, something like one of those Mallets used in the western Rockies."

West says, "Mr. O'Reily, you're not thinking big enough! The railroads, they're big thinkers, always have been!" The railroad man unveils an artist's rendering of an awesome-looking locomotive. Tom and Rachael stare at it silently. "This was designed for the 1893 Chicago World's Fair before the Pullman strike. They're working around the clock to get her in shape. We're building a special driver's seat. Yes, sir, quite a weapon."

Tom says, "Interesting choice of words, Mr. West. *Quite a weapon.* I've never seen anything like it!"

"Mr. West, the impact. What about the boilers?" Rachael asks.

"Don't worry, ma'am. We've already seen to that."

After Tom and Rachael leave, one of West's aides studies the artist's sketch of the behemoth locomotive. "Sir, with all due respect, we both know what happens when a boiler explodes. The cab gets ripped open like a tin can and the engineers are scalded alive."

"It's their duel, and it's our show!"

"Guess the audience is gonna get their money's worth," the aide says.

"The audience is going to get Bryan, and that's what we care about."

West has seen to it that, in preparation for the big event, armed guards patrol Tom's camp. The railroad constructs a huge stockade fence twenty feet high. Workmen sleep in tents within the block-square stockade. It is an armed camp operating under a blanket of top-secret security.

CHAPTER 28

Doc is with Red Eagle, talking from his train. Many workers mill about, getting the train prepared for the crash.

Doc says to Red Eagle, "Ya think Tom's engine's gonna be smashed by our train?" Red doesn't respond but keeps quietly working instead. Doc continues, "Yep, I'm certain that Tom's engine will be smashed on impact."

Doc slaps his hands together. Bam! "Aren't ya excited, Injun?"

Red Eagle remains silent, fixing some part of the train. Doc is trying not to sound too nervous. "C'mon, the whole world's gonna be watchin'. This will be our finest hour in this train! Days of dusty prairie towns and nowhere hickvilles are outta sight! Tomorrow, my half-Scot friend, you and I will be on the map! Rich and famous!"

"You will be all over the inside of the cab unless we finish the saddle, boss. We need to finish crash-proofing the cab."

Red Eagle explains the elaborate setup to Doc. "See here, boss, a series of springs that will absorb the initial impact. A special padded harness will hold you in the cab."

Doc says, "Well, quit foolin' around and finish completing this contraption."

Red straps himself in the seat and looks at the boilers with great concern. "I'm still worried about the boilers."

Doc replies, "You sure do know how to reassure a fellow." He shakes his head and walks outside.

About five hundred people are gathered around Doc's construction area. The air is heavy with drama, flecked with light touches of holiday spirit—a strange combination. Some families have brought along picnic baskets. Children romp with glee.

As Doc walks out of the cab, there are several calls for autographs and photographs. He poses for photographs beside his mighty engine and signs autographs for the spectators. "That's right, you'll be seeing my opponents' train spread all over the countryside."

One of the spectators says to Doc, "Would you oblige me with your autograph, sir?"

Doc signs the piece of paper and says, "Don't worry, partner. I'll be back 'round here tomorrow to sign more autographs."

He is basking in his overnight popularity. As far as he's concerned, the theater circuits of New York and Philadelphia are but dim lightbulbs compared to this spectacle.

Miniature locomotives, exactly like the one on Rachael's mantel, are being sold by vendors. "Come 'n' get them, for one dollar, just one dollar, o'er here, gen-u-wine soo-ve-neers, only one dollar each, certified collectors' items of miniature loco-motives soldered together in a mock collision! Get 'em for one dollar, one dollar over here."

Doc finishes his display and the signing of autographs. "I bid you farewell, my most gracious of audiences, for I have a big day ahead of me tomorrow."

William F. Cody, also known as Buffalo Bill, is the best-known spokesman for the West and is known all around the world. He goes over to the train stockade to see Doc, dressed in his ten-gallon hat and leather coat with fringes, and wearing his six-shooter. He is immediately recognized by the crowd. There is an audible whisper as people start crowding around him, saying to each other, "It's Buffalo Bill."

Buffalo Bill says to the guards, "Howdy, partner."

One of the guards asks, "Is that really you, Buffalo Bill?"

"I don't kid around about who I am."

"Sorry for questioning you. You just caught us by surprise."

"No reason to be sorry. Where can I find Doc?"

"I'll go get Red Eagle and Doc," the guard says.

Buffalo Bill says, "Where's the Injun?"

"Hold your horses. I'll go get them."

Moments later, Doc and the guard come walking toward Buffalo Bill from around the back of the train. Red Eagle is following close behind. Doc looks larger than life, proud that Buffalo Bill has come to see him personally. In his grandest showmanship style, he stretches out his hand.

Buffalo Bill says, "Pleasure to meet you, son."

"What lucky star do I thank for meeting you?"

"Wanted to see this mass of humanity myself, sonny."

Doc is a little bit uncomfortable around Bill. He hasn't really met anyone world-famous like Bill. "Sure, Bill."

"Been reading about you in all the newspapers, Doc. You're the most famous person this side of the Mississippi."

"I appreciate the compliment, but I must correct you. *You're* the most famous person on *both* sides of the Mississippi."

"I think you underestimate yourself, sonny. Ever since this 'Challenge to the Death' program started, I haven't been able to fill up my Wild West Show. Damn shame. However, I appreciate the genius of your program."

Doc smiles. "It's not really a *program*, Wild Bill. This is the real deal. One of us is going to die tomorrow."

U.S. Library of Congress

Buffalo Bill is surprised by his response. "Hey, come on, partner. This is supposed to be a show. You're joshin' me."

"Nope, this is the real deal. This is not a show. This is a duel to the death."

"In that case, you're not a genius but a damn fool. You build up all that drama, gather the folks, and boom. You're here today but gone tomorrow. You're nothing but a flash in the pan."

Red Eagle says, "Flash in the pan. I like that!"

"You must be Red Eagle," Bill says.

"You know me?"

Buffalo Bill replies, "Yes, everyone knows about you. I'd love to have you in my Wild West Show."

Red Eagle thinks about it. He doesn't know where the future leads after this event. He feels that the future is bleak for all the Indian

U.S. Library of Congress

nations. "Sorry, Mr. Buffalo Bill. I'm not doing any Western shows."

Buffalo Bill tells Red Eagle and Doc that after the event he'd like them to come to the town of Cody, which is situated in the northwest corner of Wyoming's Bighorn Basin. "Maybe you'd stage a train wreck in Cody to get people out to my new town."

Doc is happy to meet Buffalo Bill, but he's feeling overwhelmed with the amount of work that he has to do prior to the wreck. "We've got things to do," he says.

"Of course, I understand. I'm heading out to California after this show. Sure a pleasure to make your acquaintance. We'll be certain to look you up after tomorrow's event." Buffalo Bill shakes his head and walks away. He is tired of listening to fools who throw their lives away for nothing. "Nice knowing you, sonny."

Later in the day, Doc poses for more photographs beside his locomotive and signs more autographs. He loves the popularity.

A tall, young black youth comes toward Doc, a guitar under his arm. "You must be Doc." He grins. "I'm Scott Joplin." Joplin is a fine pianist, but he also plays the guitar. The young balladeer and songwriter is better known to Doc than to most people in the crowd.

"Don't tell me you're going to perform at this clambake." Doc laughs.

"Oh no, sir," Joplin replies. "But I would like to bum around this land and pick up on the spirit of what people are talking about. You know the working man's sorrow. Today they're talking about you." Joplin hands Doc a folded sheet of paper with a song he has written and dedicated to the event. "The lines aren't meant to be printed or read," Joplin explains. He begins to strum his guitar and sing. The way Scott Joplin croons, poor rhyming and faulty sentence structure doesn't matter. He sings only the last verse.

"The people came from miles around from all the ol'
cow towns. It was a delightful day it seemed, the sound
of the hissin' steam, To see the mighty steam engine,
duelin' with the other train. The whistles callin' out
with a scream, O it was a nightmarish dream. They
found him in the wreck, a-scalded to death. O Lord,
A-scalded to death by the steam."

The crowd bursts into a round of applause when he finishes. Doc stands motionless for a moment and then shakes Joplin's hand, "You're a fine songwriter, Joplin." Doc smiles at him. "But I don't mind telling you that I sure don't care for that 'scalded to death' part."

Joplin moves closer to Doc. He speaks as though the two of them are old friends. "No offense, Mr. Doc, but those words about dying. You see all those people out there? They come to see somebody die! That's the spirit I get. They want to see some blood—you and that other fella's." Doc's face grows serious as he scans the crowd of those fascinated with death. "It's all right, Mr. Doc," Joplin says. "I'll leave out the lyrics. I'll just make it a nice rag."

In the middle of the night, Red Eagle leaves the compound and walks to a fashionable hotel in Saint Louis. The town is completely quiet while everyone sleeps. He slips into the hotel unnoticed by the desk clerk and then walks down the hallway. Red Eagle's footsteps are silent. He pauses at one door and listens.

Quietly, Red Eagle forces the unlocked door open and quickly closes it behind him. He moves to the bed, and the bed's occupant stirs. Red Eagle taps her on the arm and whispers, "I am not a dream nor an eagle in the sky."

Rachael sits up in bed, startled. "Get out of here, chief!" she says without conviction.

"Need to talk."

"It's a little late for a reading lesson."

Red Eagle says, "You can't sleep; I can't sleep. Warriors, before they attack, before the kill—they don't sleep either."

Rachael snaps. "Nobody's getting killed tomorrow."

Maybe she believes it, but Red Eagle knows better. "That's what you think?"

Rachael shrugs. "I don't know about you, but Tom's train is perfectly safe."

Red Eagle sits on the side of the bed. "Hah. Doc says he's not gonna die either. Maybe they both die. Maybe just the trains die."

She folds her arms across her chest and tries to ignore him.

Red Eagle continues. "I used to watch the bighorn sheep when they would fight over the female. Two strong, brave, smart animals. You know where they fight?" Rachael doesn't answer. "They fight on the tall rocks! Hah! Not down in the grass. Not on the sand slopes. On the tallest rock, where the most danger is. You know why?" Rachael gives Red Eagle a silent, angry look. "I'll tell you why. The female sheep leads them up there. Just like you led Doc and Tom."

Rachael is mad now. "I'm not leading anyone on! This is what they chose. I live my life my way, and nobody owns me! Those two were stupid and stubborn before I was born! I don't owe them anything!" Satisfied with her outburst, Rachael is quiet.

Red Eagle thinks about her comments for a while before speaking again. "In my tribe, the eagle is more powerful than the bear. The eagle is faster than the deer. The eagle has more magic than the sun or moon. Hah! The great eagle. I'll tell you a secret. The great eagle is a slave! All he really thinks about is the nest full of skinny babies. His whole life, he worries about those baby eagles."

Red Eagle looks her straight in the face. "You gotta be a part of someone! Doc and Tom, they're someone, and tomorrow they're gonna both die."

She begins to cry, and he puts his huge hand on her shoulder, then draws her near. Rachael hugs him tight, sobbing inconsolably. She really doesn't know why. Maybe it is the loss of her youth. Whatever it is, she suddenly sees Red in a new light. "Oh, Red. You're such a great friend. You are right. It has to be stopped."

U.S. Library of Congress

He tells her, "It's too late to stop it! Those crowds, the railroad people—we couldn't stop it, even if we tried! We need the wisdom of the elders, the strength of the bear. Me, I'm like the eagle. I always worry about those baby eagles."

She starts laughing first. Then Red follows, until both of them are laughing louder and louder. Their laughter dies down, and they look at each other. He gazes longingly at her, while she still has tears in her eyes.

Rachael asks, "What are we going to do?"

"Confucius says that to see what is right and not do it is lack of courage."

"You have surpassed your teacher."

Red Eagle hesitates and then pulls Rachael in close to him. They look at each other, and then they lean in slowly and kiss.

"You're the most wise and gentle man I know," she says.

CHAPTER 29

The morning of the deadly duel arrives. The hills outside Saint Louis are blackened with thousands of spectators staking claims on viewing sites. The sideshows begin their noisy racket. Pitchmen sell their souvenirs, vendors sell food and drink. Squadrons of photographers unload their gear and assemble at the crash site. Dignitaries pose for pictures, and the railroad bosses are among those being photographed. Presidential candidate Bryan is standing up on a podium facing the crowd. A dozen balloonists hover above the milling throng, their silent crafts affording them a splendid view of the spectacle below. Bryan holds his hands to silence the crowd as they're chanting for a duel.

"Ladies and gentlemen, I welcome you wholeheartedly to today's event. But before we begin, I'd like to say a few words regarding our upcoming election."

The crowd chants, "Train wreck! Train wreck!"

Bryan shouts, "Yes, yes, we'll all get to see the crash. Because I'm like you. I want to see the crash as much as you do. I am just like you, the Great Commoner, champion of the little guy, and an avid lover of trains."

The crowd laughs and cheers for Bryan—or the train crash. It's hard to tell with the commotion going on.

"I want to place America on the silver standard to take us out of this depression; to help those in financial need; to keep America plowing ahead as a leader in the twentieth century; to aid the common man. My promise to you, if elected, is to make certain that everyone in America has a silver spoon!"

The crowd is tired of waiting. "Train wreck! Train wreck!"

Bryan tells the crowd, "Before I leave, I thank you for being here today. Remember: cast your votes for Bry—"

The crowd surges and shouts in unison, "Train wreck! Train wreck!"

Bryan's thoughts are thrown off. "Um, yes, well, vote for Bryan, the Great Commoner!"

It seems that all of Saint Louis must be present. Men, women, and children are singing, dancing, eating, and drinking in anxiety-ridden expectation. Dozens of constables on horseback form a line a hundred yards away from the crash site.

A constable is telling the crowd, "Move away. C'mon, folks, keep it clear, away from the site. C'mon now, move away." Again and again, the frenzied crowd pushes through the cordon, trying to get closer to the point of impact. The constable continues to tell the crowd to stand back, and they are ignoring him. "Stand back, folks! C'mon now, stand away, farther away."

The police move the throngs back with their horses and batons, but they are losing ground with each attempt. An officer in charge is reporting to West, who is sitting on the platform reserved for dignitaries. He tells West, "We can't hold 'em back, sir."

"All the railroad men I've talked to say the crowds are too close. I could wire for a garrison and get some troops."

West sharply replies, "Too late! You're not holding up this show for anything, Captain! You just warn those idiots, that's all!"

The crowd surges forward again. They are clapping their hands and stomping their feet. "Train wreck! Train wreck!" The crowd can hardly wait for the action to begin. They are standing a mere twenty yards from the rails.

A wild-eyed man dressed in colorful garments and wearing a shaggy gray beard parades up and down before the crowd. He carries a huge sign: Worship Not Steam Nor Steel.

It's Rachael's father. Luther says, "Go back to your homes."

The crowd moves even closer to the rails. No one is listening to him.

Red Eagle fires up Doc's engine, and the rumble of steam through the boiler builds to a mighty roar. The two-hundred-ton gladiator is ready to roll. The locomotive pulls only a coal tender, which is loaded down with slabs of lead ballast for extra weight.

Red Eagle says, "Let me help strap you into the harness seat, Doc."

"Thanks! You've been a true friend, Red."

After Doc is strapped in by the harnesses, Red Eagle slams shut the steel door to the locomotive.

Red Eagle says, "A fine day for a wreck. Good luck, partner."

"See ya in a few, Injun."

Doc releases the throttle, and the giant piston rods groan under the stress of moving the six-and-a-half-foot drive wheels. Slowly, the locomotive moves out of the work area. The crowd's cheering becomes a roar.

The locomotive moves at a walking pace to the edge of the amphitheater of humanity. People gaze at the locomotive's awesome appearance as it rolls past them, finally stopping at the point where the charge will begin.

Photographers gather around Doc's locomotive. "Doc, could ya wave to the camera for a picture?" one of the photographers asks.

Doc acknowledges the crowd, but he is watching a column of smoke rising from the enemy's secret stockade. He leans out of the cab and focuses his binoculars on the stockade. All heads turn toward the other camp, waiting for the challenger to appear. Everyone's gaze is fixed on the closed doors of the stockade.

The crowd is shouting, "Train wreck! Train wreck!"

CHAPTER 30

Hundreds in the crowd are shouting. Suddenly, the crowd's shouts are silenced with a loud roar from behind the stockade gates. Then a loud boom follows. Four mushroom clouds of smoke fill the air above the stockade, repeating the thunderous burst. There is a deafening cadence.

Red Eagle and Doc exchange unknowing glances with each other from afar. They are watching the emissions of four smokestacks. Doc says to himself, "My God, what demon have they created?"

The stunned throngs of spectators watch openmouthed as the gates open and a block-long locomotive grinds its way out of the stockade. The drive wheels are ten feet in diameter, twenty of them turning under an unbelievable hulk of moving steel. The nose of the locomotive wears an armor steel wedge, like that of a monstrous snowplow. Huge white letters on the side of the armor plate spell out the name *W. J. Bryan.*

Tom leans out of his cab, waves, and then salutes the crowd. "Thank you for coming out today."

Rachael is at his side. Tom peers down the straight line of track in Doc's direction. In a bold gesture, he salutes Doc and his engine. Doc lowers his binoculars and returns the salute. Tom sees the response and says to himself, "So long, partner."

The thousands of thrill-seeking spectators scurry back to their places. Already having seen more than they bargained for, they know that a slaughter is forthcoming. The *W. J. Bryan* dwarfs its opponent.

The two locomotives stand at opposite ends of the single track, panting like animals ready for the kill.

The mayor of Saint Louis, Cyrus Packard Walbridge, stands ready, about to give the starting signal. He looks up and down the track at both locomotives. The crowd becomes silent, knowing that the crash is just moments away.

Mayor Walbridge says, "Mr. Jennings, ladies, and gentlemen: without further ado, let the festivities begin, and may God have mercy on your souls."

The crowd cheers wildly.

CHAPTER 31

Doc is waiting patiently in the cab when Red Eagle taps him on the shoulder. Doc turns to look. "Huh? What are you doing back here?"

"I want you to meet a friend of mine." Red Eagle holds up a dummy filled with sawdust dressed in clothing identical to Doc's, complete with the goggles.

"What the heck?" Doc asks.

The chief's mighty fist smashes into his face. "Sorry, partner," Red Eagle says.

Doc collapses from his seat onto the steel floor, and the giant Indian ties his unconscious partner's hands together.

A skyrocket flies high into the sky, signaling the drivers to begin the charge.

Red Eagle jams the dummy into the harness seat and pulls the throttle wide open. "This should do it." He bends down, grabs Doc, and lifts him up. He throws the unconscious man out of the moving train, and then he jumps. They roll through the prairie brush, somersaulting in the dust.

The two monster locomotives begin to charge down the rail, whistles shrieking a spine-chilling battle cry. The rails bend and squeal under the enormous weight of the two locomotives. The trains pick up speed, racing toward each other at well over sixty miles an hour.

As each engine plows forward, torpedo signals fastened to the rails explode in rapid-fire succession, punctuating the roaring sound of the locomotives like rifle shots. The crowd lets out a battle cry in unison, knowing that the impact is but moments away. "Awwwaaaah!"

When Doc comes to, he spits dust from his mouth and curses Red Eagle. "Have you gone crazy, chief?"

Red Eagle ignores him as he carries Doc toward one of the work shanties.

"Chief, what the hell are you doing?"

Red Eagle shoves him into a waiting buckboard. "Quiet!"

Damit is pulling the buckboard, which is steered by its front wheels and carries a seat for the driver. Under the seat is a closed compartment, and Red Eagle shoves Doc into it.

"You're fired, chief."

Red Eagle slams the door shut, muffling Doc's protests. "Yeah, I know. This is a big break for your traveling show."

In a matter of seconds, the two locomotives meet. An earth-shattering roar booms through the afternoon skies. The *W. J. Bryan* splits open the front of Doc's locomotive like a piece of firewood under an ax.

Immediately, the boilers of Doc's locomotive burst open, sending two massive chunks of the engine flying through the air in the direction of the crowd. The

Locomotive boiler from Baldwin Locomotive Works – 1894 – U.S. library of Congress

crowd runs to avoid the flying debris. Armor plate rivets pop out of their moorings, peppering the crowd with deadly shrapnel. The onlookers take shelter behind covered wagons. The coal tender of Doc's train is flung end over end.

Bryan tells Forrest West, "You've got to get me out of here. This is a disaster."

West says, "Follow me."

CHAPTER 32

Scores of spectators cry out from their injuries. Thousands panic in an attempt to avoid the shower of iron and cinders. Photographers run from the site.

Four locomotive wheels roll through the crowd, find a target in the main exhibition tent, flatten the structure, and then burst into flames. The *W. J. Bryan* rolls on its side and skids through a group of spectators. The steam boilers explode in succession as Doc's engine did. A new shower of hot steel, shrapnel, and steam cover the crowd.

A reporter chases the retreating carriages of William Jennings Bryan and his aides. "Mr. Jennings, we need a comment."

Forrest West says, "Mr. Jennings will provide you with a statement tomorrow."

Fires break out everywhere. The horrified crowd of three hundred thousand people panics. Everywhere people are doing their best to take care of their wounded and dead. Both locomotives are still gushing steam. Chunks of twisted metal are lying everywhere, still red hot from the firebox coals.

Red Eagle rushes the horse-drawn buckboard to the secret stockade camp where the *W. J. Bryan* was created. He pulls the buckboard up to the stockade doors where he finds Tom lying in a clump of bushes. "It's over, Tom." He jumps off the buckboard and runs to Tom, who is tied up and gagged.

Red Eagle drags Tom to the buckboard, throws him up on the back, and covers him with a blanket. "This should stop them from recognizing you." He pulls Doc out from under the buckboard seat and throws him next to Tom.

Doc says, "You have really lost it, Injun."

"We figured that you two fools were crazy enough to kill each other," Red Eagle says and rips the gag from Tom's mouth.

Tom says, "She damn near killed me. Where is she?"

"I don't know," Red Eagle says. "Can't find her. She was supposed to meet me here. You two fools stay here."

"I'm coming with you," Doc says, getting up.

"You lie still and be quiet. If this crowd finds you two alive, they will lynch you." Red Eagle rushes back to the impact zone on foot.

Both locomotives are still gushing steam. He peers inside the cab of the *W. J. Bryan*, squinting his eyes through the black smoke and steam.

Red Eagle's eyes open wide. He reaches out and grabs a crumpled sunbonnet covered with grime. Opening it up, he finds a Paris label.

Red Eagle walks back to the waiting buckboard. His eyes are filled with tears and are wild with fear. "I told her to get out and then jump. Then, I'd get Doc out, and then jump. We were to meet by the stockade and leave this crazy place."

"Where is she?" Doc says when Red Eagle reaches them.

Tom says, "Did she ride in it herself?"

Red Eagle shakes his head. "She wasn't supposed to."

Tom and Doc look around, bewildered. They look back at Red Eagle as he produces the crumpled sunbonnet. Doc and Tom examine it painfully.

"She wore this bonnet this morning," Tom says.

The next day's early morning sun beats down on the endless alfalfa fields.

Doc is slumped over the reins of the buckboard, and Red Eagle lies sprawled out in the back. Tom sits on the end of the tailgate, staring at the dusty road moving underneath him. Red Eagle looks up and sees a wagon with two people aboard, approaching them from the rear at top speed. The wagon is about to overtake them, kicking up dust on the old road.

The rider is dressed in a multicolored outfit, his face hidden under a hat. He says in a deep voice, "You boys look lost."

Doc is afraid of being recognized and has his hat pulled over his face. "Just minding our own business."

The rider responds, "Looks like your business could be my business."

"I don't quite understand the implication, *friend*," Doc says.

The rider says, "*Implication*. That's a mighty big word for a couple of trail riders."

Red Eagle lifts his head up from the back of the wagon when he recognizes something familiar in the rider's voice. "Why don't you join a couple of entertainers for a spell?" he says.

Luther takes his hat off to show the trio his face, and Rachael takes her head covering off to show her long, hidden hair.

Luther says, "I will take you up on your offer."

Everyone is trying to put the last chain of events together. Red Eagle asks jokingly, "And who is the pretty lady next to you?"

"I'd like you to meet my daughter," Luther says.

Red Eagle says, "I'm honored, ma'am."

Doc's eyes grow wide. "Rachael, it's you?"

"Well, I'll be damned. It's impossible," Tom says as he slaps a hand on his knee.

Rachael grins. "Hey, boys. You look like you've just seen a ghost."

Doc looks at Luther, clears his throat, and says, "Nice seeing you again, sir."

"Don't worry, Doc. That's all in the past."

Tom says, "I should have put it together. I must be getting a little slower in my old age."

"I was just stopping by to see my daughter," the old gypsy says. "Thought I could lend a hand."

Doc wonders if Luther is going back to the gypsies. "Are you going ba—oh, never mind." He knows the answer before he asks the question.

"Once you are a gypsy, you are always a gypsy," says Luther. "It's in our blood. They are my family. We've turned over a new leaf. We're now selling used machinery."

Red Eagle asks, "Rachael, where were you when we were supposed to rendezvous?"

Rachael answers, "I went back to gather up some possessions we had forgotten. My father helped me." She lifts up the seat of her wagon and produces several suitcases filled with money that were left behind in the Pullman in the panic.

"The bad news," says Rachael, "is that the authorities want all of us arrested. Our train-wrecking days are over for good."

Red Eagle inclines his head toward her. "Happy that you are safe. Money doesn't make me happy. You make me happy."

Doc says, "I'm going to cash out, folks, and head out to California."

Tom nods. "I think I'm going to settle down now too and see what else comes along."

Luther says, "Rachael thought you boys would feel that way."

Rachael chuckles. "Well, I think this would be a fine time to divide up the money."

Red Eagle replies, "It was a fine show!"

She equally divides the piles of money. At this point, they have all built up enough trust that there isn't a question of it not being equal. After the cash is divided, each man shoves his portion into his saddlebags.

Doc tells the group that they should split up and find a safe place to put the cash. They know the risks of being on the road, and they understand that they are all targets if someone realizes that they are carrying a considerable amount of cash.

After they've all gone their separate ways, Red Eagle catches up with Rachael and her father. "A young woman needs assistance along the trail," he says. She only nods her head with a nearly imperceptible grin. And Red Eagle joins them on the old buckboard, smiling widely.

The balance of the William Jennings Bryan presidential campaign was nearly nonexistent, and Bryan lost the election by a landslide. W. J. Bryan was never heard from again.

CHAPTER 33

ORANGE COUNTY, CALIFORNIA, 1911

Fifteen years later on a sprawling orange tree farm, Tom is in the orange fields. Doc, who is substantially older, gets out of his black Model T Ford and walks up to Tom. "Thanks for meeting me, Tom."

Tom holds his hand out. "Great to see you again. I don't think Rachael and Red Eagle are going to meet us this time."

"It's a little more difficult with her having a child on the way."

Suddenly, a biplane crop duster swoops low over the field, fogging the thousands of acres of orange trees with a cloud of chemicals. The crop duster makes a lazy pass above the crops, this time covering the Model T Ford, Doc, and Tom with the pungent insecticide.

Another crop duster appears from behind a group of eucalyptus trees on a small hill.

The two crop dusters can't turn out of each other's way quickly enough, and they collide in midair.

Doc looks at Tom. "Are you thinking what I'm thinking?"

"Yeah!"

"We'd better get up there!"

Coughing and rubbing their eyes, Doc and Tom run to the top of the hill.

The wreckage of the two biplanes lies all over the green field. Both planes are a twisted shamble of wings and tail sections.

Incredibly, the two crop duster pilots were thrown from the planes, and they are standing there, shouting at each other.

"What's the matter with you?" one pilot says. "You could have killed us both!"

"I told you I was going to be flying lower than you, you idiot."

The two flyers continue to stand in the field and conduct a lively shouting match.

Doc and Tom scratch their heads and survey the damage.

"You know something, Doc? I would pay five dollars to see that again!"

Doc has another glorious inspiration.

CHAPTER 34

Rachael finishes her story, telling her grandchildren, Ian and Heather, that Doc went on to stage plane crashes with crop dusters. "He was killed shortly thereafter in a midair collision in Hollywood doing airplane stunts in 1912.

"I heard that Tom O'Reily went back to his life of fighting battle to battle. He enlisted as a pilot and was later killed in World War I in a dogfight over Germany in 1914. He was honored with a Medal of Honor as a flying ace, with more than thirty kills in the sky.

"Red Eagle and I fell in love and were happily married. From the moment he hugged me, I knew that I was in love with him. We settled here in Grand Forks, North Dakota. Later, your grandfather was able to hunt on his native Indian lands."

Rachael holds the wrecked-train models, gazing at them with a far-off longing. "I have no regrets. I had a wonderful life married to Red Eagle."

The End

Red Eagle & General Jackson – U.S. Library of Congress

Red Eagle and his squaw – 1924 Herbert A. French – U.S. Library of Congress

APPENDIX

HISTORICAL FIGURES

William Jennings Bryan was born March 19, 1860, and died July 26, 1925. In 1896 Bryan ran an unsuccessful bid for president of the United States. A former Democratic congressman from Nebraska, he gained his party's presidential nomination in July of that year after his electrifying "Cross of Gold" speech at the Democratic National Convention. He ran against Grover Cleveland.

Buffalo Bill Cody was born February 26, 1846, and died January 10, 1917. He was an American soldier, bison hunter, and showman. He was born in the city of Le Claire in what was then known as the Iowa Territory, resided in Canada as a child, and then moved with his family to the Kansas Territory. Buffalo Bill received the Medal of Honor in 1872 for service to the US Army as a scout. He became famous for his American Old West cowboy shows.

The Dalton Gang consisted of real brothers: Frank, Grat, Bob, and Emmett Dalton. They were also known as the "Wild Bunch."

Scott Joplin was born in 1868 and died April 1, 1917. He was a black songwriter famous for ragtime.

William "Red Eagle" Weatherford is a true historical figure. He was six feet four inches tall. He was called Billy in his early years. He was the son of Charles Weatherford, a Scottish trader. His uncle was Alexander McGillivray, who became important in the Creek Confederacy during the Revolutionary War.

Since he was only one-half Scottish, he was a half-breed in the eyes of the law, an outcast of the white man. But since power in their tribe was given through the mother's side of the family, Red Eagle held a high-ranking position. His father married a Creek Indian princess squaw in the Oklahoma Territories and fought beside the Indians to help them try to achieve their independence. He had a nasty habit of burning and derailing trains.

Red Eagle became a leader of the Red Sticks, militant Indians who fought against whites who were taking the tribes' lands. Red Eagle led a raid on Fort Mims in which more than five hundred whites were killed. General Andrew Jackson fought Red Eagle near Talladega, Alabama. Davy Crockett was with Jackson during this fight. The Red Sticks lost the battle, but Red Eagle was able to escape by riding his horse off a high cliff into the deep river below. The rest of the Red Sticks were killed. He was responsible for the Fort Mims massacre in 1814.

Red Eagle later walked into General Jackson's camp at Fort Toulouse and surrendered, asking nothing for himself. He requested only that his woman and children be retrieved from the woods where they were hiding out and starving. The general was so impressed with Red Eagle's bravery that he placed him under his protection. Red Eagle died in 1824 and is buried beside his mother, Sehoy Tate Weatherford.

My children are distant relatives of Red Eagle through the Weatherfords.

ABOUT THE AUTHOR

David Rosten has been involved in "Indian Princesses" over the years. His Indian name is Red Eagle. His children's great-grandmother Ione West was a distant relation of Red Eagle. He is a community director for the Center for Citizenbuilding, Department of Social Sciences, at the University of California, and he is on the national board of directors of the Olive Tree Initiative at UC Irvine. He is former cochair of the Dean's Council at UC Irvine and currently lives in Newport Beach with his children.

David Rosten is the author of five previous books: *Olaf's Saga: The True Story of a Viking King and the Discovery of America*; *The Dragon's Triangle: The True Story of the First Nonstop Flight Across the Pacific*; *The Last Cheetah: A Narrative History of Egyptian Royalty from 1805 to 1953*; and *The Last Romantic: The True Story of the Life of Enrique Granados* and a fictional book called *The Hermitage*.